AGATHA CHRISTIE

Endless Night

PUBLISHED BY POCKET  BOOKS NEW YORK

ENDLESS NIGHT

Dodd, Mead edition published 1968

POCKET BOOK edition published March, 1969

7th printing....................November, 1974

L

This POCKET BOOK edition includes every word contained in the original, higher-priced edition. It is printed from brand-new plates made from completely reset, clear, easy-to-read type. POCKET BOOK editions are published by POCKET BOOKS, a division of Simon & Schuster, Inc., 630 Fifth Avenue, New York, N.Y. 10020. Trademarks registered in the United States and other countries.

Cheryl Tyminski   10/9/75

"FORGET ABOUT GIPSY'S ACRE,"
whined the old crone.

"There's none that'll get any good out of Gipsy's Acre. They'd do best to leave it alone." She nodded vigorously and then she repeated to herself, "There's no luck for them as meddles with Gipsy's Acre. There never has been."

"What happened in the house?" I asked. "Why has it been empty so long? Why was it left to fall down?"

"I don't gossip about Gipsy's Acre," was her answer; but then she dropped her voice to add, "I'll tell your fortune—

"If you ever return to Gipsy's Acre, you'll return to sorrow and loss and danger. There's trouble, black trouble, waiting for you. Forget you ever saw this place!"

ENDLESS NIGHT
was originally published by
Dodd, Mead & Company, Inc.

Books by Agatha Christie

The A.B.C. Murders
A Caribbean Mystery
A Murder Is Announced
A Pocket Full of Rye
And Then There Were None
At Bertram's Hotel
The Body in the Library
By the Pricking of My Thumbs
Cat Among the Pigeons
The Clocks
Crooked House
Dead Man's Folly
Death Comes as the End
Easy to Kill (Original British title: Murder Is Easy)
Endless Night
Evil Under the Sun
Funerals Are Fatal
Hallowe'en Party
Hickory Dickory Death (Original British title: Hickory, Dickory, Dock)
The Mirror Crack'd (Original British title: The Mirror Crack'd from Side to Side)

Mrs. McGinty's Dead
Murder in the Calais Coach (Original British title: Murder on the Orient Express)
The Murder of Roger Ackroyd
Murder with Mirrors (Original British title: They Do It with Mirrors)
The Mystery of the Blue Train
Nemesis
The Pale Horse
Passenger to Frankfurt
Peril at End House
Remembered Death (Original British title: Sparkling Cyanide)
So Many Steps to Death (Original British title: Destination Unknown)
Third Girl
Towards Zero
What Mrs. McGillicuddy Saw (Original British title: 4:50 from Paddington)

Published by POCKET BOOKS

Every Night and every Morn
Some to Misery are born.
Every Morn and Every Night
Some are born to Sweet Delight,
Some are born to Sweet Delight,
Some are born to Endless Night.

WILLIAM BLAKE
Auguries of Innocence

ENDLESS NIGHT

BOOK ONE

1

In my end is my beginning. . . . That's a quotation I've often heard people say. It sounds all right—but what does it really mean?

Is there ever any particular spot where one can put one's finger and say, "It all began that day, at such a time and such a place, with such an incident"?

· Did my story begin, perhaps, when I noticed the sale bill hanging on the wall of the George and Dragon announcing sale by auction of that valuable property "The Towers," and giving particulars of the acreage, the miles and furlongs, and the highly idealized portrait of The Towers as it might have been perhaps in its prime, anything from eighty to a hundred years ago.

I was doing nothing particular, just strolling along the main street of Kingston Bishop, a place of no importance whatever, killing time. I noticed the sale bill. Why? Fate up to its dirty work? Or dealing out its golden handshake of good fortune? You can look at it either way.

Or you could say, perhaps, that it all had its beginnings

when I met Santonix, during the talks I had with him; I can close my eyes and see his flushed cheeks, the over-brilliant eyes, and the movement of the strong yet delicate hand that sketched and drew plans and elevations of houses. One house in particular, a beautiful house, a house that would be wonderful to own!

My longing for a house, a fine and beautiful house, such a house as I could never hope to have, flowered into life then. It was a happy fantasy shared between us, the house that Santonix would build for me—if he lasted long enough . . .

A house that in my dream I would live in with the girl that I loved, a house in which just like a child's silly fairy story we should live together "happy ever afterward." All pure fantasy, all nonsense, but it stated that tide of longing in me—longing for something I was never likely to have.

Or if this is a love story—and it is a love story, I swear —then why not begin where I first caught sight of Ellie standing in the dark fir trees of Gipsy's Acre?

Gipsy's Acre. Yes, perhaps I'd better begin there, at the moment when I turned away from the sale board with a little shiver because a black cloud had come over the sun, and asked a question carelessly enough of one of the locals, who was clipping a hedge in a desultory fashion nearby.

"What's this house, The Towers, like?"

I can still see the queer face of the old man as he looked at me sideways and said,

"That's not what us calls it here. What sort of a name is that?" He snorted disapproval. "It's many a year now since folks lived in it and called it The Towers." He snorted again.

I asked him then what he called it, and again his eyes shifted away from me in his old wrinkled face in that queer way country folk have of not speaking to you direct, looking over your shoulder or round the corner, as it were, as though they saw something you didn't; and he said,

"It's called hereabouts Gipsy's Acre."

"Why is it called that?" I asked.

"Some sort of a tale. I dunno rightly. One says one thing, one says another." And then he went on, "Anyway, it's where the accidents take place."

"Car accidents?"

"All kinds of accidents. Car accidents mainly nowadays. It's a nasty corner there, you see."

"Well," I said, "if it's a nasty curve, I can well see there might be accidents."

"Rural council put up a danger sign, but it don't do no good, that don't. There are accidents just the same."

"Why Gipsy?" I asked him.

Again his eyes slipped past me and his answer was vague.

"Some tale or other. It was gipsies' land once, they say, and they were turned off, and they put a curse on it."

I laughed.

"Aye," he said, "you can laugh, but there's places as *is* cursed. You smart alecks in town don't know about them. But there's places as is cursed, all right, and there's a curse on this place. People got killed here in the quarry when they got the stone out to build. Old Geordie, he fell over the edge there one night and broke his neck."

"Drunk?" I suggested.

"He may have been. He liked his drop, he did. But there's many drunks as fall—nasty falls—but it don't do them no lasting harm. But Geordie, he got his neck broke. In there," he pointed up behind him to the pine-covered hill, "in Gipsy's Acre."

Yes, I suppose that's how it began. Not that I paid much attention to it at the time. I just happened to remember it. That's all. I think—that is, when I think properly—that I built it up a bit in my mind. I don't know if it was before or later that I asked if there were still any gipsies about there. He said there weren't many anywhere nowadays. The police were always moving them on, he said. I asked,

"Why doesn't anybody like gipsies?"

"They're a thieving lot," he said disapprovingly. Then he peered more closely at me. "Happen you've got gipsy blood yourself?" he suggested, looking hard at me.

3

I said not that I knew of. It's true; I do look a bit like a gipsy. Perhaps that's what fascinated me about the name of Gipsy's Acre. I thought to myself as I was standing there smiling back at him, amused by our conversation, that perhaps I had a bit of gipsy blood.

Gipsy's Acre. I went up the winding road that led out of the village and wound up through the dark trees and came at last to the top of the hill so that I could see out to sea and the ships. It was a marvelous view and I thought, just as one does think things, "I wonder how it would be if Gipsy's Acre was my acre?"—just like that. It was only a ridiculous thought. When I passed my hedge clipper again, he said,

"If you want gipsies, there's old Mrs. Lee, of course. The Major, he give her a cottage to live in."

"Who's the Major?" I asked.

He said in a shocked voice, "Major Phillpot, of course." He seemed quite upset that I should ask! I gathered that Major Phillpot was God locally. Mrs. Lee was some kind of dependent of his, I suppose, whom he'd provided for. The Phillpots seemed to have lived there all their lives and more or less to run the place.

As I wished my old boy good day and turned away, he said,

"She's got the last cottage at the end of the street. You'll see her outside, maybe. Doesn't like the inside of houses Them as has got gipsy blood don't."

So there I was, wandering down the road, whistling and thinking about Gipsy's Acre. I'd almost forgotten what I'd been told when I saw a tall black-haired old woman staring at me over a garden hedge. I knew at once it must be Mrs. Lee. I stopped and spoke to her.

"I hear you can tell me all about Gipsy's Acre up there," I said.

She stared at me through a tangled fringe of black hair and she said,

"Don't have nought to do with it, young man. You listen to me. Forget about it. You're a good-looking lad. Nothing good comes out of Gipsy's Acre and never will."

"I see it's up for sale," I said.

"Aye, that's so, and more fool he who buys it."

"Who's likely to buy it?"

"There's a builder after it. More than one. It'll go cheap. You'll see."

"Why should it go cheap?" I asked curiously. "It's a fine site."

She wouldn't answer that.

"Supposing a builder buys it cheap; what will he do with it?"

She chuckled to herself. It was malicious, unpleasant laughter.

"Pull down the old ruined house and build, of course. Twenty—thirty houses, maybe—and all with a curse on them."

I ignored the last part of the sentence. I said, speaking before I could stop myself,

"That would be a shame. A great shame."

"Ah, you needn't worry. They'll get no joy of it, not those who buys and not those who lays the bricks and mortar. There'll be a foot that slips on the ladder, and there'll be the lorry that crashes with a load, and the slate that falls from the roof of a house and finds its mark. And the trees, too. Crashing, maybe, in a sudden gale. Ah, you'll see! There's none that'll get any good out of Gipsy's Acre. They'd do best to leave it alone. You'll see. You'll see." She nodded vigorously and then she repeated softly to herself, *"There's no luck for them as meddles with Gipsy's Acre.* There never has been."

I laughed. She spoke sharply.

"Don't laugh, young man. It comes to me as may be one of these days you'll laugh on the wrong side of your mouth. There's never been no luck there, not in the house nor yet in the land."

"What happened in the house?" I asked. "Why has it been empty so long? Why was it left to fall down?"

"The last people that lived there died, all of them."

"How did they die?" I asked out of curiosity.

"Best not to speak of it again. But no one cared to come and live in it afterward. It was left to molder and decay. It's forgot by now and best that it should be."

5

"But you could tell me the story," I said wheedlingly. "You know all about it."

"I don't gossip about Gipsy's Acre." Then she let her voice drop to a kind of phony beggar's whine. "I'll tell your fortune now, my pretty lad, if you like. Cross my palm with silver and I'll tell your fortune. You're one of those that'll go far one of these days."

"I don't believe that nonsense about fortunetelling," I said, "and I haven't any silver. Not to spare, anyway."

She came nearer to me and went on in a wheedling voice. "Sixpence now. Sixpence now. I'll do it for sixpence. What's that? Nothing at all. I'll do it for sixpence because you're a handsome lad with a ready tongue and a way with you. It could be that you'll go far."

I fished a sixpence out of my pocket, not because I believed in any of her foolish superstitions but because for some reason I liked the old fraud even if I did see through her. She grabbed the coin from me and said,

"Give me your hand then. Both hands."

She took my hands in her withered claw and stared down at the open palms. She was silent for a minute or two, staring. Then she dropped my hands abruptly, almost pushing them away from her. She retreated a step and spoke harshly.

"If you know what's good for you, you'll get out of Gipsy's Acre here and now and you won't come back! That's the best advice I can give you. Don't come back."

"Why not? Why shouldn't I come back?"

"Because if you do, you'll come back to sorrow and loss and danger maybe. There's trouble, black trouble, waiting for you. Forget you ever saw this place. I'm warning you."

"Well, of all the—"

But she had turned away and was retreating to the cottage. She went in and slammed the door. I'm not superstitious. I believe in luck, of course, who doesn't? But not a lot of superstitious nonsense about ruined houses with curses on them. And yet I had an uneasy feeling that the sinister old creature had seen something in my hands. I looked down at my two palms spread out in front of me.

What could anyone see in the palms of anyone's hands?
Fortunetelling was arrant nonsense—just a trick to get
money out of you—money out of your silly credulity. I
looked up at the sky. The sun had gone in, the day seemed
different now. A sort of shadow, a kind of menace. Just
an approaching storm, I thought. The wind was beginning
to blow, the backs of the leaves were showing on the trees.
I whistled to keep my spirits up and walked along the
road through the village.

I looked again at the pasted-up bill advertising the auction of The Towers. I even made a note of the date. I had
never attended a property sale in my life, but I thought to
myself that I'd come and attend this one. It would be interesting to see who bought The Towers—that is to say,
interesting to see who became the owner of Gipsy's Acre.
Yes, I think that's really where it all began. . . . A fantastic notion occurred to me. I'd come and pretend to myself that I was the man who was going to bid for Gipsy's
Acre! I'd bid against the local builders! They'd drop out,
disappointed in their hopes of buying it cheap. I'd buy it
and I'd go to Rudolf Santonix and say, "Build me a
house. I've bought the site for you." And I'd find a girl, a
wonderful girl, and we'd live in it together happy ever
after.

I often had dreams of that kind. Naturally they never
came to anything, but they were fun. That's what I
thought then. Fun! Fun, my God! If I'd only known!

2

It was pure chance that had brought me to the neighborhood of Gipsy's Acre that day. I was driving a hire car,
taking some people down from London to attend a sale—
a sale not of a house but of its contents. It was a big house
just at the outskirts of the town, a particularly ugly one.

I drove an elderly couple there who were interested, from what I could overhear of their conversation, in a collection of papier-mâché, whatever papier-mâché was. The only time I ever heard it mentioned before was by my mother in connection with washing-up bowls. She'd said that a papier-mâché washing-up bowl was far better than a plastic one any day! It seemed an odd thing for rich people to want to come down and buy a collection of the stuff.

However, I stored the fact away in my mind and I thought I would look in a dictionary or read up somewhere what papier-mâché really was. Something that people thought worthwhile to hire a car for, and go down to a country sale and bid for. I liked knowing about things. I was twenty-two years of age at that time and I had picked up a fair amount of knowledge one way and another. I knew a good deal about cars, was a fair mechanic and a careful driver. Once I'd worked with horses in Ireland. I nearly got entangled with a dope gang, but I got wise and quit in time. A job as a chauffeur to a classy car hire firm isn't bad at all. Good money to be made with tips. And not usually too strenuous. But the work itself was boring.

Once I'd gone fruit picking in summertime. That didn't pay much, but I enjoyed myself. I'd tried a lot of things. I'd been a waiter in a third-class hotel, life guard on a summer beach, I'd sold encyclopedias and vacuum cleaners and a few other things. I'd once done horticultural work in a botanical garden and had learned a little about flowers.

I never stuck to anything. Why should I? I'd found nearly everything I did interesting. Some things were harder work than others, but I didn't really mind that. I'm not really lazy. I suppose what I really am is restless. I want to go everywhere, see everything, do everything. I want to find something. Yes, that's it. I want to find something.

From the time I left school I wanted to find something, but I didn't yet know what that something was going to be. It was just something I was looking for in a vague, unsatisfied sort of way. It was somewhere. Sooner or later I'd know all about it. It might perhaps be a girl. . . . I like girls, but no girl I'd met so far had been important. . . . You liked them all right, but then you went on to the next one quite gladly. They were like the jobs I took. All right for a bit, and then you got fed up with them and you wanted to move on to the next one. I'd gone from one thing to another ever since I'd left school.

A lot of people disapproved of my way of life. I suppose they were what you might call my well-wishers. That was because they didn't understand the first thing about me. They wanted me to go steady with a nice girl, save money, get married to her and then settle down to a nice steady job. Day after day, year after year, world without end, amen. Not for yours truly! There must be something better than that. Not just all this tame security, the good old welfare state limping along in its half-baked way! Surely, I thought, in a world where man has been able to put satellites in the sky and where men talk big about visiting the stars, there must be something that rouses you, that makes your heart beat, that's worthwhile searching all over the world to find! One day, I remember, I was walking down Bond Street. It was during my waiter period and I was due on duty. I'd been strolling, looking at some shoes in a shop window. Very natty they were. Like they say in the advertisements in newspapers: *What smart men are wearing today* and there's usually a picture of the smart man in question. My word, he usually looks a twerp! Used to make me laugh, advertisements like that did.

I passed on from the shoes to the next window. It was a picture shop. Just three pictures in the window artily arranged with a drape of limp velvet in some neutral color arranged over a corner of a gilt frame. Cissy, if you know what I mean. I'm not much of a one for art. I dropped in to the National Gallery once out of curiosity. Fair gave me the pip, it did. Great big shiny colored pictures of battles in rocky glens, or emaciated saints getting themselves stuck with arrows. Portraits of simpering great ladies sitting smirking in silks and velvets and lace. I decided then and there that art wasn't for me. But the picture I was looking at now was somehow different. There were three pictures in the window. One a landscape, nice bit of country for what I call every day. One of a woman drawn in such a funny way, so much out of proportion, that you could hardly see she was a woman. I suppose that's what they call *art nouveau*. I don't know what it was about. The third picture was my picture. There wasn't really much to it, if you know what I mean. It was—how can I describe it? It was kind of simple. A lot of space in it and a few great widening circles all round each other, if you can put it that way. All in different colors—odd colors that you wouldn't expect. And here and there, there were sketchy bits of color that didn't seem to mean anything. Only somehow they did mean something! I'm no good at description. All I can say is that one wanted terribly to go on looking at it.

I just stood there, feeling queer, as though something very unusual had happened to me. Those fancy shoes now, I'd have liked them to wear. I mean I take quite a bit of trouble about my clothes. I like to dress well so as to make an impression, but I never seriously thought in my life of buying a pair of shoes in Bond Street. I know the kind of fancy prices they ask there—fifteen pounds a pair, those shoes might be. Handmade or something, they call it, making it more worthwhile, for some reason. Sheer waste of money that would be. A classy line in shoes, yes, but you can pay too much for class. I've got my head screwed on the right way.

But this picture, what would that cost, I wondered? Suppose I were to buy that picture? You're crazy, I said to myself. You don't go for pictures, not in a general way. That was true enough. But I wanted this picture. . . . I'd like it to be mine. I'd like to be able to hang it and sit and look at it as long as I liked and know that I owned it! Me! Buying pictures. It seemed a crazy idea. I took a look at the picture again. Me wanting that picture didn't make sense, and anyway, I probably couldn't afford it. Actually

I was in funds just at that moment. A lucky tip on a horse. This picture would probably cost a packet. Twenty pounds? Twenty-five? Anyway, there would be no harm in asking. They couldn't eat me, could they? I went in, feeling rather aggressive and on the defensive.

The inside of the place was all very hushed and grand. There was a sort of muted atmosphere, with neutral color walls and a velvet settee on which you could sit and look at the pictures. A man who looked a little like the model for the perfectly dressed man in advertisements came and attended to me, speaking in a rather hushed voice to match the scenery. Funnily, he didn't look superior as they usually do in high-grade Bond Street shops. He listened to what I said and then he took the picture out of the window and displayed it for me against a wall, holding it there for me to look at as long as I wanted. It came to me then —in the way you sometimes know just exactly how things are, that the same rules didn't apply to pictures as they do about other things. Someone might come into a place like this dressed in shabby old clothes and a frayed shirt and turn out to be a millionaire who wanted to add to his collection. Or he could come in looking cheap and flashy. rather like me, perhaps, but somehow or other he'd got such a yen for a picture that he managed to get the money together by some kind of sharp practice.

"A very fine example of the artist's work," said the man who was holding the picture.

"How much?" I said briskly.

The answer took my breath away.

"Twenty-five thousand," he said in his gentle voice.

I'm quite good at keeping a poker face. I didn't show anything. At least I don't think I did. He added some name that sounded foreign. The artist's name, I suppose, and that it had just come on the market from a house in the country, where the people who lived there had had no idea what it was. I kept my end up and sighed.

"It's a lot of money, but it's worth it, I suppose," I said.

Twenty-five thousand pounds. What a laugh!

"Yes," he said, and sighed. "Yes, indeed." He lowered the picture very gently and carried it back to the window.

He looked at me and smiled. "You have good taste," he said.

I felt that in some way he and I understood each other. I thanked him and went out into Bond Street.

3

I don't know much about writing things down—not, I mean, in the way a proper writer would do. The bit about that picture I saw, for instance. It doesn't really have anything to do with anything. I mean, nothing came of it, it didn't lead to anything and yet I feel somehow that it is important, that it has a place somewhere. It was one of the things that happened to me that meant something. Just like Gipsy's Acre meant something to me. Like Santonix meant something to me.

I haven't really said much about him. He was an architect. Of course, you'll have gathered that. Architects are another thing I'd never had much to do with, though I knew a few things about the building trade. I came across Santonix in the course of my wanderings. It was when I was working as a chauffeur, driving the rich around places. Once or twice I drove abroad, twice to Germany —I knew a bit of German—and once or twice to France— I had a smattering of French, too—and once to Portugal. They were usually elderly people who had money and bad health in about equal quantities.

When you drive people like that around, you begin to think that money isn't so hot, after all. What with incipient heart attacks, lots of bottles of little pills you have to take all the time, and losing your temper over the food or the service in hotels. Most of the rich people I've known have been fairly miserable. They've got their worries, too. Taxation and investments. You hear them talking together or to friends. Worry! That's what's killing half of them. And their sex life's not so hot either. They've either got long-legged blonde sexy wives who are playing them up with boy friends somewhere, or they're married to the complaining kind of woman, hideous as hell, who keeps telling them where they get off. No. I'd rather be myself —Michael Rogers, seeing the world and getting off with good-looking girls when he feels like it!

Everything a bit hand-to-mouth, of course, but I put up with that. Life was good fun, and I'd been content to go on with life being fun. But I suppose I would have, in any case. That attitude goes with youth. When youth begins to pass, fun isn't fun any longer.

Behind it, I think, was always the other thing—wanting someone and something. . . . However, to go on with what I was saying, there was one old boy I used to drive down to the Riviera. He'd got a house being built there. He went down to look how it was getting on. Santonix was the architect. I don't really know what nationality Santonix was. English I thought at first, though it was a funny sort of name I'd never heard before. But I don't think he was English. Scandinavian of some kind, I guess. He was an ill man. I could see that at once. He was young and very fair and thin, with an odd face—a face that was askew somehow. The two sides of it didn't match. He could be quite bad-tempered to his clients. You'd have thought that since they were paying the money, that they'd call the tune and do the bullying. That wasn't so. Santonix bullied *them,* and he was always quite sure of himself although they weren't.

This particular old boy of mine was frothing with rage, I remember, as soon as he arrived and had seen how things were going. I used to catch snatches here and there when I was standing by ready to assist in my chauffeurly and handyman way. It was always on the cards that Mr. Constantine would have a heart attack or a stroke.

"You have not done as I said," he half screamed. "You have spent too much money. Much too much money. It is not as we agreed. It is going to cost me more than I thought?"

13

"You're absolutely right," said Santonix. "But the money's got to be spent."

"It shall not be spent! It shall not be spent. You have got to keep within the limits I laid down. You understand?"

"Then you won't get the kind of house you want," said Santonix. "I know what you want. The house I build you will be the house you want. I'm quite sure of that and you're quite sure of it, too. Don't give me any of your pettifogging middle-class economies. You want a house of quality and you're going to get it, and you'll boast about it to your friends and they'll envy you. I don't build a house for anyone, I've told you that. There's more to it than money. This house isn't going to be like other people's houses!"

"It is going to be terrible. Terrible."

"Oh, no, it isn't. The trouble with you is that you don't know what you want. Or at least so anyone might think. But you do know what you want really, only you can't bring it out into your mind. You can't see it clearly. But I know. That's the one thing I always know—what people are after and what they want. There's a feeling in you for quality. I'm going to give you quality."

He used to say things like that. And I'd stand by and listen. Somehow or other I could see for myself that this house that was being built there among pine trees looking over the sea wasn't going to be the usual house. Half of it didn't look out toward the sea in a conventional way. It looked inland, up to a certain curve of the mountains, up to a glimpse of sky between the hills. It was odd and unusual and very exciting.

Santonix used to talk to me sometimes when I was off duty. He said,

"I only build houses for people I want to build for."

"Rich people, you mean?"

"They have to be rich or they couldn't pay for the houses. But it's not the money I'm going to make out of it I care about. My clients have to be rich because I want to make the kind of houses that cost money. The house only isn't enough, you see. It has to have the setting. That's just as important. It's like a ruby or an emerald. A beautiful stone is only a beautiful stone. It doesn't lead you anywhere further. It doesn't mean anything, it has no form or significance until it has its setting. And the setting has to have a beautiful jewel to be worthy of. I take the setting, you see, out of the landscape, where it exists only in its own right. It has no meaning until there is my house sitting proudly like a jewel within its grasp." He looked at me and laughed. "You don't understand?"

"I suppose not," I said slowly, "and yet—in a way—I think I do. . . ."

"That may be." He looked at me curiously.

We came down to the Riviera again later. By then the house was nearly finished. I won't describe it because I couldn't do it properly, but it was—well—something special—and it was beautiful. I could see that. It was a house you'd be proud of, proud to show to people, proud to look at yourself, proud to be in with the right person, perhaps. And then suddenly one day Santonix said to me,

"I could build a house for you, you know. I'd know the kind of house you'd want."

I shook my head.

"I shouldn't know myself," I said honestly.

"Perhaps you wouldn't. I'd know for you." Then he added, "It's a thousand pities you haven't got the money."

"And never shall have," I said.

"You can't say that," said Santonix. "Born poor doesn't mean you've got to stay poor. Money's queer. It goes where it's wanted."

"I'm not sharp enough," I said.

"You're not ambitious enough. Ambition hasn't woken up in you, but it's there, you know."

"Oh, well," I said, "someday when I've woken up ambition and I've made money, then I'll come to you and say, 'Build me a house.' "

He sighed then. He said,

"I can't wait. . . . No, I can't afford to wait. I've only a short time to go now. One house—two houses more. Not more than that. One doesn't want to die young. . . . Sometimes one has to. . . . It doesn't really matter, I suppose."

15

"I'll have to wake up my ambition quick."

"No," said Santonix. "You're healthy, you're having fun. Don't change your way of life."

I said, "I couldn't if I tried."

I thought that was true then. I liked my way of life and I was having fun and there was never anything wrong with my health. I've driven a lot of people who've made money, who've worked hard, and who've got ulcers and coronary thrombosis and many other things as a result of working hard. I didn't want to work hard. I could do a job as well as another, but that was all there was to it. And I hadn't got ambition, or I didn't think I had ambition. Santonix had had ambition, I suppose. I could see that designing houses and building them, the planning of the drawing and something else that I couldn't quite get hold of, all that had taken it out of him. He hadn't been a strong man to begin with. I had a fanciful idea sometimes that he was killing himself before his time by the work he had put out to drive his ambition. I didn't want to work. It was as simple as that. I distrusted work, disliked it. I thought it was a very bad thing that the human race had unfortunately invented for itself.

I thought about Santonix quite often. He intrigued me almost more than anyone I knew. One of the oddest things in life, I think, is the things one remembers. One chooses to remember, I suppose. Something in one must choose. Santonix and his house were one of the things, and the picture in Bond Street and visiting that ruined house The Towers and hearing the story of Gipsy's Acre—all those were the things that I'd chosen to remember! Sometimes girls that I met, and journeys to the foreign places in the course of driving clients about. The clients were all the same—dull. They always stayed at the same kind of hotels and ate the same kind of unimaginative food.

I still had that queer feeling in me of waiting for something, waiting for something to be offered to me, or to happen to me, I don't quite know which way describes it best. I suppose really I was looking for a girl, the right sort of girl—by which I don't mean a nice, suitable girl to settle down with, which is what my mother would have meant

16

or my Uncle Joshua or some of my friends. I didn't know at that time anything about love. All I knew about was sex. That was all anybody of my generation seemed to know about. We talked about it too much, I think, and heard too much about it and took it too seriously. We didn't know—any of my friends or myself—what it was really going to be when it happened. Love, I mean. We were young and virile and we looked the girls over we met and we appreciated their curves and their legs and the kind of eye they gave you, and you thought to yourself: "Will they or won't they? Should I be wasting my time?" And the more girls you made, the more you boasted and the finer fellow you were thought to be, and the finer fellow you thought yourself.

I'd no real idea that that wasn't all there was to it. I suppose it happens to everyone sooner or later and it happens suddenly. You don't think as you imagine you're going to think: "This might be the girl for me. . . . This is the girl who is going to be mine." At least, I didn't feel it that way. I didn't know that when it happened it would happen quite suddenly. That I would say: "That's the girl I belong to. I'm hers. I belong to her, utterly, for always." No. I never dreamed it would be like that. Didn't one of the old comedians say once—wasn't it one of his stock jokes?—"I've been in love once, and if I felt it coming on again, I tell you I'd emigrate." It was the same with me. If I had known, if I had only known what it could all come to mean, I'd have emigrated too! If I'd been wise, that is.

4

■

I hadn't forgotten my plan of going to the auction.

There was three weeks to go. I'd had two more trips to the Continent—one to France and the other to Germany. It was when I was in Hamburg that things came to a crisis.

For one thing, I took a violent dislike to the man and his wife I was driving. They represented everything I disliked most. They were rude, inconsiderate, unpleasant to look at, and I suppose they developed in me a feeling of being unable to stand this life of sycophancy any longer. I was careful, mind you. I thought I couldn't stand them another day, but I didn't tell them so. No good running yourself in bad with the firm that employs you. So I telephoned up their hotel, said I was ill, and I wired London saying the same thing. I said I might be in quarantine and it would be advisable if they sent out a driver to replace me. Nobody could blame me for that. They wouldn't care enough about me to make further inquiries, and they'd merely think that I was too feverish to send them any more news. Later, I'd turn up in London again, spinning them a yarn of how ill I'd been! But I didn't think I should do that. I was fed up with the driving racket.

That rebellion of mine was an important turning point in my life. Because of that and of other things, I turned up at the auction rooms on the appointed date.

"Unless sold before by private treaty" had been pasted across the original board. But it was still there, so it hadn't been sold by private treaty. I was so excited I hardly knew what I was doing.

As I say, I had never been to a public auction of property before. I was imbued with the idea that it would be exciting, but it wasn't exciting. Not in the least. It was one of the most moribund performances I have ever attended. It took place in a semi-gloomy atmosphere, and there were only about six or seven people there. The auctioneer was quite different from those auctioneers that I had seen presiding at furniture sales or things of that kind—men with facetious voices and very hearty and full of jokes. This one, in a dead and alive voice, praised the property and described the acreage and a few things like that and then he went half-heartedly into the bidding. Somebody made a bid of £5,000. The auctioneer gave a tired smile rather as one who hears a joke that isn't really funny. He made a few remarks and there were a few more bids. They were mostly country types standing around. Someone who looked like a farmer, someone who I guessed to be one of the competitive builders, a couple of lawyers, I think, one a man who looked as though he was a stranger from London, well dressed and professional-looking. I don't know if he made an actual bid; he may have done. If so, it was very quietly and done more by gesture. Anyway, the bidding petered to an end, the auctioneer announced in a melancholy voice that the reserve price had not been reached, and the thing broke up.

"That was a dull business," I said to one of the country-looking fellows whom I was next to as I went out.

"Much the same as usual," he said. "Been to many of these?"

"No," I said, "actually it's the first."

"Come out of curiosity, did you? I didn't notice you doing any bidding."

"No fear," I said. "I just wanted to see how it would go."

"Well, it's the way it runs very often. They just want to see who's interested, you know."

I looked at him inquiringly.

"Only three of 'em in it, I should say," said my friend. "Whetherby from Helminster. He's the builder, you know. Then Dakham and Coombe, bidding on behalf of some Liverpool firm, I understand, and a dark horse from London, too, I should say a lawyer. Of course there may be more in it than that, but those seemed the main ones to me. It'll go cheap. That's what everyone says."

"Because of the place's reputation?" I asked.

"Oh, you've heard about Gipsy's Acre, have you? That's only what the country people say. Rural council ought to have altered that road years ago—it's a death trap."

"But the place has got a bad reputation?"

"I tell you that it's just superstition. Anyway, as I say, the real business'll happen now behind the scenes, you know. They'll go and make offers. I'd say the Liverpool people might get it. I don't think Whetherby'll go high enough. He likes buying cheap. Plenty of properties coming into the market nowadays for development. After all, it's not many people who could afford to buy the place, pull that ruined house down and put up another house there, could they?"

"Doesn't seem to happen very often nowadays," I said.

"Too difficult. What with taxation and one thing and another, and you can't get domestic help in the country. No, people would rather pay thousands for a luxury flat in a town nowadays up on the sixteenth floor of a modern building. Big unwieldy country houses are a drag in the market."

"But you could build a modern house," I argued. "Labor-saving."

"You could, but it's an expensive business, and people aren't so fond of living lonely."

"Some people might be," I said.

He laughed and we parted. I walked along frowning, puzzling to myself. My feet took me without my really noticing where I was going along the road between the trees and up, up to the curving road that led between the trees to the moorlands.

And so I came to the spot in the road where I first saw Ellie. As I said, she was standing just by a tall fir tree and she had the look, if I can so explain it, of someone who hadn't been there a moment before but had just materialized, as it were, out of the tree. She was wearing a sort of dark green tweed, and her hair was the soft brown color of an autumn leaf, and there was something a bit unsubstantial about her. I saw her and I stopped. She was looking at me, her lips just parted, looking slightly startled. I suppose I looked startled, too. I wanted to say something and I didn't quite know what to say. Then I said,

"Sorry. I—I didn't mean to startle you. I didn't know there was anyone here."

She said, and her voice was very soft and gentle, it might have been a little girl's voice but not quite. She said,

"It's quite all right. I mean, I didn't think anyone would be here either." She looked a little round her and said, "It —it's a lonely spot." And she shivered just a little.

There was rather a chilly wind that afternoon. But perhaps it wasn't the wind. I don't know. I came a step or two nearer.

"It is a sort of scary place rather, isn't it?" I said. "I mean, the house being a ruin the way it is."

"The Towers," she said thoughtfully. "That was the name of it, wasn't it, only—I mean, there don't seem to have been any towers."

"I expect that was just a name," I said. "People call their houses names like The Towers to make them sound grander than they are."

She laughed just a little. "I suppose that was it," she said. "This—perhaps you know, I'm not sure—this is the place that they're selling today or putting up for auction?"

"Yes," I said. "I've come from the auction now."

"Oh." She sounded startled. "Were you—are you—interested?"

"I'm not likely to buy a ruined house with a few hundred acres of woodland land," I said. "I'm not in that class."

"Was it sold?" she asked.

"No, it didn't come up to the reserve."

"Oh. I see." She sounded relieved.

"You didn't want to buy it either, did you?" I said.

"Oh, no," she said, "of course not." She sounded nervous about it.

I hesitated and then I blurted out the words that came to my lips.

"I'm pretending," I said. "I can't buy it, of course, because I haven't got any money, but I'm interested. I'd like to buy it. I want to buy it. Open your mouth and laugh at me if you like, but that's the way it is."

"But isn't it rather too decrepit, too—"

"Oh, yes," I said. "I don't mean I want it like it is now. I want to pull this down, cart it all away. It's an ugly house and I think it must have been a sad house. But this place isn't sad or ugly. It's beautiful. Look here. Come a little this way, through the trees. Look out at the view that way where it goes to the hills and the moors. D'you see? Clear away a vista here—and then you come this way—"

I took her by the arm and led her to a second point of

the compass. If we were behaving unconventionally, she did not notice it. Anyway, it wasn't that kind of way I was holding her. I wanted to show her what I saw.

"Here," I said, "here you see where it sweeps down to the sea and where the rocks show out there. There's a town between us and that, but we can't see it because of the hills bulging out further down the slope. And then you can look a third way, to a vague foresty valley. Do you see now if you cut down trees and make big vistas and clear this space round the house, do you see what a beautiful house you could have here? You wouldn't site it where the old one is. You'd go about fifty—a hundred yards to the right, here. This is where you could have a house, a wonderful house. A house built by an architect who's a genius."

"Do you know any architects who are geniuses?" She sounded doubtful.

"I know one," I said.

Then I started telling her about Santonix. We sat down side by side on a fallen tree and I talked. Yes, I talked to that slender woodland girl whom I'd never seen before and I put all I had into what I was telling her. I told her the dream that one could build up.

"It won't happen," I said; "I know that. It couldn't happen. But think. Think into it just like I'm thinking into it. There we'd cut the trees and there we'd open up, and we'd plant things, rhododendrons and azaleas, and my friend Santonix would come. He'd cough a good deal because I think he's dying of consumption or something, but he could do it. He could do it before he died. He could build the most wonderful house. You don't know what his houses are like. He builds them for very rich people, and they have to be people who want the right thing. I don't mean the right thing in the conventional sense. Things people who want a dream come true want. Something wonderful."

"I'd want a house like that," said Ellie. "You make me see it, feel it. . . . Yes, this would be a lovely place to live. Everything one has dreamed of come true. One could live here and be free, not hampered, not tied round by people

22

pushing you into doing everything you don't want, keeping you from doing anything you do want. Oh, I am so sick of my life and the people who are round me and everything!"

That's the way it began, Ellie and I together. Me with my dream and she with her revolt against her life. We stopped talking and looked at each other.

"What's your name?" she said.

"Mike Rogers," I said. "Michael Rogers," I amended. "What's yours?"

"Fenella." She hesitated and then said, "Fenella Goodman," looking at me with a rather troubled expression.

This didn't seem to take us much farther, but we went on looking at each other. We both wanted to see each other again—but just for the moment we didn't know how to set about it.

5

Well, that's how it began between Ellie and myself. It didn't really go along so very quickly, I suppose, because we both had our secrets. Both had things we wanted to keep from the other, and so we couldn't tell each other as much about ourselves as we might have done, and that kept bringing us up sharp, as it were, against a kind of barrier. We couldn't bring things into the open and say, "When shall we meet again? Where can I find you? Where do you live?" Because, you see, if you ask the other person that, they'd expect you to tell the same.

Fenella looked apprehensive when she gave me her name. So much so that I thought for a moment that it mightn't be her real name. I almost thought that she might have made it up! But of course I knew that that was impossible. I'd given her my real name.

We didn't know quite how to take leave of each other that day. It was awkward. It had become cold and we wanted to wander down from The Towers—but what then? Rather awkwardly, I said tentatively,

"Are you staying round here?"

She said she was staying in Market Chadwell. That was a market town not very far away. It had, I knew, a large hotel, three-starred. She'd be staying there, I guessed. She said, with something of the same awkwardness, to me,

"Do you live here?"

"No," I said, "I don't live here. I'm only here for the day."

Then a rather awkward silence fell again. She gave a faint shiver. A cold little wind had come up.

"We'd better walk," I said, "and keep ourselves warm. Are you—have you got a car or are you going by bus or train?"

She said she'd left a car in the village.

"But I'll be quite all right," she said.

She seemed a little nervous. I thought perhaps she wanted to get rid of me but didn't quite know how to manage it. I said,

"We'll walk down, shall we, just as far as the village."

She gave me a quick grateful look then. We walked slowly down the winding road on which so many car accidents had happened. As we came round a corner, a figure stepped suddenly from beneath the shelter of the fir tree. It appeared so suddenly that Ellie gave a start and said "Oh!" It was the old woman I had seen the other day in her own cottage garden—Mrs. Lee. She looked a great deal wilder today, with a tangle of black hair blowing in the wind and a scarlet cloak round her shoulders; the commanding stance she took up made her look taller.

"And what would you be doing, my dears?" she said. "What brings you to Gipsy's Acre?"

"Oh," Ellie said, "we aren't trespassing, are we?"

"That's as may be. Gipsies' land this used to be. Gipsies' land and they drove us off it. You'll do no good here, and no good will come to you prowling about Gipsy's Acre."

There was no fight in Ellie; she wasn't that kind. She said gently and politely,

"I'm very sorry if we shouldn't have come here. I thought this place was being sold today."

"And bad luck it will be to anyone who buys it!" said the old woman. "You listen, my pretty, for you're pretty enough, bad luck will come to whoever buys it. There's a curse on this land, a curse put on it long ago, many years ago. You keep clear of it. Don't have nought to do with Gipsy's Acre. Death it will bring you, and danger. Go away home across the sea and don't come back to Gipsy's Acre. Don't say I didn't warn you."

With a faint spark of resentment Ellie said,

"We're doing no harm."

"Come now, Mrs. Lee," I said, "don't frighten this young lady."

I turned in an explanatory way to Ellie.

"Mrs. Lee lives in the village. She's got a cottage there. She tells fortunes and prophesies the future. All that, don't you, Mrs. Lee?" I spoke to her in a jocular way.

"I've got the gift," she said simply, drawing her gipsy-like figure up straighter still. "I've got the gift. It's born in me. We all have it. I'll tell your fortune, young lady. Cross my palm with silver and I'll tell your fortune for you."

"I don't think I want my fortune told."

"It'd be a wise thing to do. Know something about the future. Know what to avoid, know what's coming to you if you don't take care. Come now, there's plenty of money in your pocket. Plenty of money. I know things it would be wise for you to know."

I believe the urge to have one's fortune told is almost invariable in women. I've noticed it before with girls I knew. I nearly always had to pay for them to go into the fortune-tellers' booths if I took them to a fair. Ellie opened her bag and laid two half crowns in the old woman's hand.

"Ah, my pretty, that's right now. You hear what old Mother Lee will tell you."

Ellie drew off her glove and laid her small delicate palm

in the old woman's hand. She looked down at it, muttering to herself. "What do I see now? What do I see?"

Suddenly she dropped Ellie's hand abruptly.

"I'd go away from here if I were you. Go—and don't come back! That's what I told you just now, and it's true. I've seen it again in your palm. Forget Gipsy's Acre, forget you ever saw it. And it's not just the ruined house up there; it's the land itself that's cursed."

"You've got a mania about that," I said roughly. "Anyway, the young lady has nothing to do with the land here. She's only here for a walk today; she's nothing to do with this neighborhood."

The old woman paid no attention to me. She said dourly,

"I'm telling you, my pretty. I'm warning you. You can have a happy life—but you must avoid danger. Don't come to a place where there's danger or where there's a curse. Go away where you're loved and taken care of and looked after. You've got to keep yourself safe. Remember that. Otherwise—otherwise—" she gave a short shiver—"I don't like to see it. I don't like to see what's in your hand."

Suddenly, with a queer, brisk gesture she pushed back the two half crowns into Ellie's palm, mumbling something we could hardly hear. It sounded like "It's cruel. It's cruel, what's going to happen." Turning, she stalked away at a rapid pace.

"What a—what a frightening woman," said Ellie.

"Pay no attention to her," I said gruffly. "I think she's half off her head anyway. She just wants to frighten you off. They've got a sort of feeling, I think, about this particular piece of land."

"Have there been accidents here? Have bad things happened?"

"Bound to be accidents. Look at the curve and the narrowness of the road. The town council ought to be shot for not doing something about it. Of course there'll be accidents here. There aren't enough signs warning you."

"Only accidents—or other things?"

"Look here," I said, "people like to collect disasters.

There are plenty of disasters always to collect. That's the way stories build themselves up about a place."

"Is that one of the reasons why they say this property which is being sold will go cheap?"

"Well, it may be, I suppose. Locally, that is. But I don't suppose it'll be sold locally. I expect it'll be bought for developing. You're shivering," I said. "Don't shiver. Come on, we'll walk fast." I added, "Would you rather I left you before you got back into the town?"

"No. Of course not. Why should I?"

I made a desperate plunge.

"Look here," I said, "I shall be in Market Chadwell tomorrow. I—I suppose—I don't know whether you'll still be there . . . I mean, would there be any chance of—seeing you?" I shuffled my feet and turned my head away. I got rather red, I think. But if I didn't say something now, how was I going to go on with this?

"Oh, yes," she said, "I shan't be going back to London until the evening."

"Then perhaps—would you—I mean, I suppose it's rather cheek—"

"No, it isn't."

"Well, perhaps you'd come and have tea at a café—the Blue Dog, I think it's called. It's quite nice," I said. "It's —I mean, it's—" I couldn't get hold of the word I wanted and I used the word that I'd heard my mother use once or twice—"it's quite ladylike," I said anxiously.

Then Ellie laughed. I suppose it sounded rather peculiar nowadays.

"I'm sure it'll be very nice," she said. "Yes. I'll come. About half-past four. Will that be right?"

"I'll be there waiting for you," I said. "I—I'm glad." I didn't say what I was glad about.

We had come to the last turn of the road where the houses began.

"Good-by, then," I said, "till tomorrow. And—don't think again about what that old hag said. She just likes scaring people, I think. She's not all there," I added.

"Do you feel it's a frightening place?" Ellie asked.

"Gipsy's Acre? No, I don't," I said. I said it perhaps a

27

trifle too decidedly, but I didn't think it was frightening. I thought as I'd thought before, that it was a beautiful place, a beautiful setting for a beautiful house. . . .

Well, that's how my first meeting with Ellie went. I was in Market Chadwell the next day waiting in the Blue Dog and she came. We had tea together and we talked. We still didn't say much about ourselves, nor about our lives, I mean. We talked mostly about things we thought, and felt; and then Ellie glanced at her wrist watch and said she must be going because her train to London left at five-thirty.

"I thought you had a car down here," I said.

She looked slightly embarrassed then and she said no, no, that hadn't been her car yesterday. She didn't say whose it had been. That shadow of embarrassment came over us again. I raised a finger to the waitress and paid the bill, then I said straight out to Ellie,

"Am I—am I ever going to see you again?"

She didn't look at me; she looked down at the table. She said,

"I shall be in London for another fortnight."

I said,

"Where? How?"

We made a date to meet in Regent's Park in three days' time. It was a fine day. We had some food in the open-air restaurant and we walked in Queen Mary's garden and we sat there in two deck chairs and we talked. From that time on we began to talk about ourselves. I'd had some good schooling, I told her, but otherwise I didn't amount to much. I told her about the jobs I'd had, some of them, at any rate, and how I'd never stuck to things and how I'd been restless and wandered about trying this and that. Funnily enough, she was entranced to hear all this.

"So different," she said, "so wonderfully different."

"Different from what?"

"From me."

"You're a rich girl?" I said.

"Yes," she said, "I'm a poor little rich girl."

She talked then in a fragmentary way about her background of riches, of stifling comfort, of boredom, of not really choosing your own friends, of never doing what you wanted—sometimes looking at people who seemed to be enjoying themselves, when she wasn't. Her mother had died when she was a baby and her father had married again. And then, not many years after, he had died, she said. I gathered she didn't care much for her stepmother. She'd lived mostly in America but also traveling abroad a fair amount.

It seemed fantastic to me, listening to her, that any girl in this age and time could live this sheltered, confined existence. True, she went to parties and entertainments, but it might have been fifty years ago, it seemed to me, from the way she talked. There didn't seem to be any intimacy, any fun! Her life was as different from mine as chalk from cheese. In a way it was fascinating to hear about it, but it sounded stultifying to me.

"You haven't really got any friends of your own then?" I said incredulously. "What about boy friends?"

"They're chosen for me," she said rather bitterly. "They're deadly dull."

"It's like being in prison," I said.

"That's what it seems like."

"And really no friends of your own?"

"I have now. I've got Greta."

"Who's Greta?" I said.

"She came first as an *au pair* girl—no, not quite that, perhaps. But anyway I'd had a French girl who lived with us for a year, for French, and then Greta came from Germany, for German. Greta was different. Everything was different once Greta came."

"You're very fond of her?" I asked.

"She helps me," said Ellie. "She's on my side. She arranges so that I can do things and go places. She'll tell lies for me. I couldn't have got away to come down to Gipsy's Acre if it hadn't been for Greta. She's keeping me company and looking after me in London while my stepmother's in Paris. I write two or three letters and if I go off anywhere, Greta posts them every three or four days so that they have a London postmark."

"Why did you want to go down to Gipsy's Acre, though?" I asked. "What for?"

She didn't answer at once.

"Greta and I arranged it," she said. "She's rather wonderful," she went on. "She thinks of things, you know. She suggests ideas."

"What's this Greta look like?" I asked.

"Oh, Greta's beautiful," she said. "Tall and blonde. She can do anything."

"I don't think I'd like her," I said.

Ellie laughed.

"Oh, yes, you would. I'm sure you would. She's very clever, too."

"I don't like clever girls," I said. "And I don't like tall blonde girls. I like small girls with hair like autumn leaves."

"I believe you're jealous of Greta," said Ellie.

"Perhaps I am. You're very fond of her, aren't you?"

"Yes, I am very fond of her. She's made all the difference in my life."

"And it was she suggested you come down here. Why, I wonder? There's not much to see or do in this part of the world. I find it rather mysterious."

"It's our secret," said Ellie, and looked embarrassed.

"Yours and Greta's? Tell me."

She shook her head. "I must have some secrets of my own," she said.

"Does your Greta know you're meeting me?"

"She knows I'm meeting someone. That's all. She doesn't ask questions. She knows I'm happy."

After that there was a week when I didn't see Ellie. Her stepmother had come back from Paris, also someone whom she called Uncle Frank, and she explained almost casually that she was having a birthday, and that they were giving a big party for her in London.

"I shan't be able to get away," she said. "Not for the next week. But after that—after that, it'll be different."

"Why will it be different after that?"

"I shall be able to do what I like then."

"With Greta's help, as usual?" I said.

It used to make Ellie laugh the way I talked about Greta. She'd say, "You're so silly to be jealous of her. One day you must meet her. You'll like her."

"I don't like bossy girls," I said obstinately.

"Why do you think she's bossy?"

"By the way you talk about her. She's always busy arranging something."

"She's very efficient," said Ellie. "She arranges things very well. That's why my stepmother relies on her so much."

I asked what her Uncle Frank was like.

She said, "I don't know him really so very well. He was my father's sister's husband, not a real relation. I think he's always been rather a rolling stone and got into trouble once or twice. You know the way people talk about someone and sort of hint things."

"Not socially acceptable?" I asked. "Bad lot?"

"Oh, nothing really bad, I think, but he used to get into scrapes, I believe. Financial ones. And trustees and lawyers and people used to have to get him out of them. Pay up for things."

"That's it," I said. "He's the bad hat of the family. I expect I'd get on better with him than I would with the paragon Greta."

"He can make himself very agreeable when he likes," said Ellie. "He's good company."

"But you don't really like him?" I asked sharply.

"I think I do. . . . It's just that sometimes, oh, I can't explain it. I just feel I don't know what he's thinking or planning."

"One of our planners, is he?"

"I don't know what he's really like," said Ellie again.

She didn't ever suggest that I should meet any of her family. I wondered sometimes if I ought to say something about it myself. I didn't know how she felt about the subject. I asked her straight out at last.

"Look here, Ellie," I said, "do you think I ought to—meet your family, or would you rather I didn't?"

"I don't want you to meet them," she said at once.

"I know I'm not much—" I said.

31

"I don't mean it that way, not a bit! I mean they'd make a fuss. I can't stand a fuss."

"I sometimes feel," I said, "that this is rather a hole-and-corner business. It puts me in a rather bad light, don't you think?"

"I'm old enough to have my own friends," said Ellie. "I'm nearly twenty-one. When I am twenty-one, I can have my own friends and nobody can stop me. But now you see—well, as I say, there'd be a terrible fuss and they'd cart me off somewhere so that I couldn't meet you. There'd be—oh, do, do let's go on as we are now."

"Suits me if it suits you," I said. "I just didn't want to be, well, too underhand about everything."

"It's not being underhand. It's just having a friend one can talk to and say things to. It's someone one can—" she smiled suddenly—"one can make believe with. You don't know how wonderful that is."

Yes, there was a lot of that—make-believe! More and more our times together were to turn out that way. Sometimes it was me. More often it was Ellie who'd say, "Let's suppose that we've bought Gipsy's Acre and that we're building a house there."

I had told her a lot about Santonix and about the houses he'd built. I tried to describe to her the kind of houses they were and the way he thought about things. I don't think I described it very well, because I'm not good at describing things. Ellie, no doubt, had her own picture of the house—our house. We didn't say "our house," but we knew that's what we meant. . . .

So for over a week I wasn't to see Ellie. I had taken out what savings I had (there weren't many), and I'd bought her a little green shamrock ring made of some Irish bog stone. I'd given it to her for a birthday present and she'd loved it and looked very happy.

"It's beautiful," she said.

She didn't wear much jewelry and when she did, I had no doubt it was real diamonds and emeralds and things like that, but she liked my Irish green ring.

"It will be the birthday present I like best," she said.

Then I got a hurried note from her. She was going

abroad with her family to the South of France immediately after her birthday.

"But don't worry," she wrote, "we shall be back again in two or three weeks' time, on our way to America this time. But anyway, we'll meet again then. I've got something special I want to talk to you about."

I felt restless and ill at ease not seeing Ellie and knowing she'd gone abroad to France. I had a bit of news about the Gipsy's Acre property, too. Apparently it had been sold by private treaty, but there wasn't much information about who'd bought it. Some firm of London solicitors apparently were named as the purchasers. I tried to get more information about it, but I couldn't. The firm in question were very cagey. Naturally I didn't approach the principals. I palled up to one of their clerks and so got a little vague information. It had been bought for a very rich client who was going to hold it as a good investment capable of appreciation when the land in that part of the country was becoming more developed.

It's very hard to find out about things when you're dealing with really exclusive firms. Everything is as much of a deadly secret as though they were M.I.5 or something! Everyone is always acting on behalf of someone else who can't be named or spoken of! Takeover bids aren't in it!

I got into a terrible state of restlessness. I stopped thinking about it all and I went and saw my mother.

I hadn't seen her for a good long time.

6

My mother lived in the same street she had lived in for the last twenty years—a street of drab houses all highly respectable and devoid of any kind of beauty or interest. The front doorstep was nicely whitened and it looked just the same as usual. It was No. 46. I pressed the front doorbell. My mother opened the door and stood there looking at me. She looked just the same as usual, too. Tall and angular, gray hair parted in the middle, mouth like a rat-trap, and eyes that were eternally suspicious. She looked hard as nails. But where I was concerned, there was a core of softness somewhere in her. She never showed it, not if she could help it, but I'd found out that it was there. She'd never stopped for a moment wanting me to be different, but her wishes were never going to come true. There was a perpetual state of stalemate between us.

"Oh," she said, "so it's you."

"Yes," I said, "it's me."

She drew back a little to let me pass, and I came into the house and went on past the sitting-room door and into the kitchen. She followed me and stood looking at me.

"It's been quite a long time," she said. "What have you been doing?"

I shrugged my shoulders.

"This and that," I said.

"Ah," said my mother, "as usual, eh?"

"As usual," I agreed.

"How many jobs have you had since I saw you last?"

I thought a minute. "Five," I said.

"I wish you'd grow up."

"I'm fully adult," I said. "I have chosen my way of life. How have things been with you?" I added.

"Also as usual," said my mother.

"Quite well and all that?"

"I've no time to waste being ill," said my mother. Then she said abruptly, "What have you come for?"

"Should I have come for anything in particular?"

"You usually do."

"I don't see why you should disapprove so strongly of my seeing the world," I said.

"Driving luxurious cars all over the Continent! Is that your idea of seeing the world?"

"Certainly."

"You won't make much of a success in that. Not if you throw up the job at a day's notice and go sick, dumping your clients in some heathen town."

34

"How did you know about that?"

"Your firm rang up. They wanted to know if I knew your address."

"What did they want me for?"

"They wanted to reemploy you, I suppose," said my mother. "I can't think why."

"Because I'm a good driver and the clients like me. Anyway, I couldn't help it if I went sick, could I?"

"I don't know," said my mother.

Her view clearly was that I could have helped it.

"Why didn't you report to them when you got back to England?"

"Because I had other fish to fry," I said.

She raised her eyebrows. "More notions in your head? More wild ideas? What jobs have you been doing since?"

"Petrol pump. Mechanic in a garage. Temporary clerk, washer-up in a sleazy night-club restaurant."

"Going down the hill, in fact," said my mother with a kind of grim satisfaction.

"Not at all," I said. "It's all part of the plan. My plan!"

She sighed. "What would you like, tea or coffee? I've got both."

I plumped for coffee. I've grown out of the tea drinking habit. We sat there with our cups in front of us and she took a homemade cake out of a tin and cut us each a slice.

"You're different," she said suddenly.

"Me, how?"

"I don't know, but you're different. What's happened?"

"Nothing's happened. What should have happened?"

"You're excited," she said.

"I'm going to rob a bank," I said.

She was not in the mood to be amused. She merely said,

"No, I'm not afraid of your doing that."

"Why not? Seems a very easy way of getting rich quickly nowadays."

"It would need too much work," she said. "And a lot of planning. More brain work than you'd like to have to do. Not safe enough, either."

35

"You think you know all about me," I said.

"No, I don't. I don't really know anything about you, because you and I are as different as chalk and cheese. But I know when you're up to something. You're up to something now. What is it, Micky? Is it a girl?"

"Why should you think it's a girl?"

"I've always known it would happen someday."

"What do you mean by 'someday'? I've had lots of girls."

"Not the way I mean. It's only been the way of a young man with nothing to do. You've kept your hand in with girls, but you've never been really serious till now."

"But you think I'm serious now?"

"Is it a girl, Micky?"

I didn't meet her eyes. I looked away and said, "In a way."

"What kind of a girl is she?"

"The right kind for me," I said.

"Are you going to bring her to see me?"

"No," I said.

"It's like that, is it?"

"No, it isn't. I don't want to hurt your feelings, but—"

"You're not hurting my feelings. You don't want me to see her in case I should say to you 'Don't.' Is that it?"

"I wouldn't pay any attention if you did."

"Maybe not, but it would shake you. It would shake you somewhere inside, because you take notice of what I say and think. There are things I've guessed about you —and maybe I've guessed right and you know it. I'm the only person in the world who can shake your confidence in yourself. Is this girl a bad lot who's got hold of you?"

"Bad lot?" I said, and laughed. "If you only saw her! You make me laugh."

"What do you want from me? You want something. You always do."

"I want some money," I said.

"You won't get it from me. What do you want it for— to spend on this girl?"

"No," I said, "I want to buy a first-class suit to get married in."

"You're going to marry her?"

"If she'll have me."

That shook her.

"If you'd only tell me something!" she said. "You've got it badly, I can see that. It's the thing I always feared, that you'd choose the wrong girl."

"Wrong girl! Hell!" I shouted. I was angry.

I went out of the house and I banged the door.

7

When I got home, there was a telegram waiting for me—it had been sent from Antibes.

Meet me tomorrow four-thirty usual place.

Ellie was different. I saw it at once. We met as always in Regent's Park and at first we were a bit strange and awkward with each other. I had something I was going to say to her and I was in a bit of a state as to how to put it. I suppose any man is when he comes to the point of proposing marriage.

And she was strange about something, too. Perhaps she was considering the nicest and kindest way of saying No to me. But somehow I didn't think that. My whole belief in life was based on the fact that Ellie loved me. But there was a new independence about her, a new confidence in herself which I could hardly feel was simply because she was a year older. One more birthday can't make that difference to a girl. She and her family had been in the South of France and she told me a little about it. And then rather shyly she said,

"I—I saw that house there, the one you told me about. The one that architect friend of yours had built."

"What—Santonix?"

"Yes. We went there to lunch one day."

37

"How did you do that? Does your stepmother know the man who lives there?"

"Dmitri Constantine? Well—not exactly, but she met him and—well—Greta fixed it up for us to go there as a matter of fact."

"Greta again," I said, allowing the usual exasperation to come into my voice.

"I told you," she said, "Greta is very good at arranging things."

"Oh, all right. So she arranged that you and your stepmother—"

"And Uncle Frank," said Ellie.

"Quite a family party," I said, "and Greta, too, I suppose."

"Well, no, Greta didn't come because, well—" Ellie hesitated—"Cora, my stepmother, doesn't treat Greta exactly like that."

"She's not one of the family, she's a poor relation, is she?" I said. "Just the *au pair* girl, in fact. Greta must resent being treated that way sometimes."

"She's not an *au pair* girl; she's a kind of companion to me."

"A chaperon," I said, "a cicerone, a duenna, a governess. There are lots of words."

"Oh, do be quiet," said Ellie, "I want to tell you. I know now what you mean about your friend Santonix. It's a wonderful house. It's—it's quite different. I can see that if he built a house for us it would be a wonderful house."

She had used the words quite unconsciously. Us, she had said. She had gone to the Riviera and had made Greta arrange things so as to see the house I had described, because she wanted to visualize more clearly the house that we would, in the dream world we'd built for ourselves, have built for us by Rudolf Santonix.

"I'm glad you felt like that about it," I said.

She said: "What have you been doing?"

"Just my dull job," I said, "and I've been to a race meeting and I put some money on an outsider. Thirty to one. I put every penny I had on it and it won by a length. Who says my luck isn't in?"

"I'm glad you won," said Ellie, but she said it without excitement, because putting all you had in the world on an outsider, and the outsider winning, didn't mean anything in Ellie's world. Not the kind of thing it meant in mine.

"And I went to see my mother," I added.

"You've never spoken much of your mother."

"Why should I?" I said.

"Aren't you fond of her?"

I considered. "I don't know," I said. "Sometimes I don't think I am. After all, one grows up and—outgrows parents. Mothers and fathers."

"I think you do care about her," said Ellie. "You wouldn't be so uncertain when you talk about her otherwise."

"I'm afraid of her in a way," I said. "She knows me too well. She knows the worst of me, I mean."

"Somebody has to," said Ellie.

"What do you mean?"

"There's a saying by some great writer or other that no man is a hero to his valet. Perhaps everyone ought to have a valet. It must be hard otherwise, always living up to people's good opinion of one."

"Well, you certainly have ideas, Ellie," I said. I took her hand. "Do you know all about me?" I said.

"I think so," said Ellie. She said it quite calmly and simply.

"I never told you much."

"You mean you never told me anything at all; you always clammed up. That's different. But I know quite well what you are like, you yourself."

"I wonder if you do," I said. I went on, "It sounds rather silly saying I love you. It seems too late for that, doesn't it? I mean, you've known about it a long time, practically from the beginning, haven't you?"

"Yes," said Ellie, "and you knew, too, didn't you, about me?"

"The thing is," I said, "what are we going to do about it? It's not going to be easy, Ellie. You know pretty well what I am, what I've done, the sort of life I've led. I went back to see my mother and the grim respectable little street she lives in. It's not the same world as yours, Ellie. I don't know that we can ever make them meet."

"You could take me to see your mother."

"Yes, I could," I said, "but I'd rather not. I expect that sounds very harsh to you, perhaps cruel, but you see we've got to lead a queer life together, you and I. It's not going to be the life that you've led and it's not going to be the life that I've led either. It's got to be a new life where we have a sort of meeting ground between my poverty and ignorance and your money and culture and social knowledge. My friends will think you're stuck-up and your friends will think I'm socially unpresentable. So what are we going to do?"

"I'll tell you," said Ellie, "exactly what we're going to do. We're going to live on Gipsy's Acre in a house—a dream house—that your friend Santonix will build for us. That's what we're going to do." She added, "We'll get married first. That's what you mean, isn't it?"

"Yes," I said, "that's what I mean. If you're sure it's all right for you."

"It's quite easy," said Ellie; "we can get married next week. I'm of age. you see. I can do what I like now. That makes all the difference. I think perhaps you're right about relations. I shan't tell my people and you won't tell your mother, not until it's all over and then they can throw fits and it won't matter."

"That's wonderful," I said, "wonderful, Ellie. But there's one thing. I hate telling you about it. We can't live at Gipsy's Acre, Ellie. Wherever we build our house, it can't be there because it's sold."

"I know it's sold," said Ellie. She was laughing. "You don't understand, Mike. I'm the person who's bought it."

8

I sat there on the grass by the stream among the water flowers with the little paths and the stepping stones all round us. A good many other people were sitting round about us, but we didn't notice them or even see they were there, because we were like all the others—a young couple talking about their future. I stared at her and stared at her. I just couldn't speak.

"Mike," she said. "There's something, something I've got to tell you. Something about me, I mean."

"You don't need to," I said; "no need to tell me anything."

"Yes, but I must. I ought to have told you long ago, but I didn't want to because—because I thought it might drive you away. But it explains, in a way, about Gipsy's Acre."

"You bought it?" I said. "But how did you buy it?"

"Through lawyers," she said, "the usual way. It's a perfectly good investment, you know. The land will appreciate. My lawyers were quite happy about it."

It was odd suddenly to hear Ellie, the gentle and timid Ellie, speaking with such knowledge and confidence of the business world of buying and selling.

"You bought it for us?"

"Yes. I went to a lawyer of my own, not the family one. I told him what I wanted to do, I got him to look into it, I got everything set up and in train. There were two other people after it, but they were not really desperate and they wouldn't go very high. The important thing was that the whole thing had to be set up and arranged ready for me to sign as soon as I came of age. It's signed and finished."

"But you must have made some deposit or something beforehand. Had you enough money to do that?"

"No," said Ellie, "no, I hadn't control of much money beforehand, but of course there are people who will advance you money. And if you go to a new firm of legal advisers, they will want you to go on employing them for business deals once you've come into what money you're going to have, so they're willing to take the risk that you might drop down dead before your birthday comes."

"You sound so businesslike," I said, "you take my breath away!"

"Never mind business," said Ellie. "I've got to get back to what I'm telling you. In a way I've told it you already, but I don't suppose really you realize it."

"I don't want to know," I said. My voice rose, I was almost shouting. "Don't tell me anything. I don't want to know anything about what you've done or who you've been fond of or what has happened to you."

"It's nothing of that kind," she said. "I didn't realize that that was what you were fearing it might be. No, there's nothing of that kind. No sex secrets. There's nobody but you. The thing is that I'm—well—I'm rich."

"I know that," I said; "you've told me already."

"Yes," said Ellie with a faint smile, "and that's what you said to me, 'poor little rich girl.' But in a way it's more than that. My grandfather, you see, was enormously rich. Oil. Mostly oil. And other things. The wives he paid alimony to are dead, there was only my father and myself left because his other two sons were killed. One in Korea and one in a car accident. And so it was all left in a great big huge trust and when my father died suddenly, it all came to me. My father had made provision for my stepmother before, so she didn't get anything more. It was all mine. I'm—actually one of the richest women in America, Mike."

"Good Lord," I said. "I didn't know . . . Yes, you're right, I didn't know it was like that."

"I didn't want you to know. I didn't want to tell you. That was why I was afraid when I said my name—Fenella Goodman. We spell it G-u-t-e-m-a-n, and I thought you might know the name of Guteman, so I slurred over it and made it into Goodman."

"Yes," I said, "I've seen the name of Guteman vaguely. But I don't think I'd have recognized it even then. Lots of people are called names rather like that."

"That's why," she said, "I've been so hedged around all the time and fenced in and imprisoned. I've had detectives guarding me and young men being checked before they're allowed even to speak to me. Whenever I've made a friend, they've had to be quite sure it wasn't an unsuitable one. You don't know what a terrible, terrible prisoner's life it is! But now that's all over, and if you don't mind—"

"Of course I don't mind," I said; "we shall have lots of fun. In fact," I said, "you couldn't be too rich a girl for me!"

We both laughed. She said: "What I like about you is that you can be natural about things."

"Besides," I said, "I expect you pay a lot of tax on it, don't you? That's one of the few nice things about being like me. Any money I make goes into my pocket and nobody can take it away from me."

"We'll have our house," said Ellie, "our house on Gipsy's Acre." Just for a moment she gave a sudden little shiver.

"You're not cold, darling," I said. I looked up at the sunshine.

"No," she said.

It was really very hot. We'd been basking. It might almost have been the South of France.

"No," said Ellie, "it was just that—that woman, that gipsy that day."

"Oh, don't think of her," I said. "She was crazy anyway."

"Do you think she really thinks there's a curse on the land?"

"I think gipsies are like that. You know—always wanting to make a song and dance about some curse or something."

"Do you know much about gipsies?"

"Absolutely nothing," I said truthfully. "If you don't want Gipsy's Acre, Ellie, we'll buy a house somewhere else. On the top of a mountain in Wales, on the coast of

43

Spain or an Italian hillside, and Santonix can build us a house there just as well."

"No," said Ellie, "that's how I want it to be. It's where I first saw you walking up the road, coming round the corner very suddenly, and then you saw me and stopped and stared at me. I'll never forget that."

"Nor will I," I said.

"So that's where it's going to be. And your friend Santonix will build it."

"I hope he's still alive," I said with an uneasy pang. "He was a sick man."

"Oh, yes," said Ellie, "he's alive. I went to see him."

"You went to see him?"

"Yes. When I was in the South of France. He was in a sanatorium there."

"Every minute, Ellie, you seem to be more and more amazing. The things you do and manage."

"He's rather a wonderful person, I think," said Ellie, "but rather frightening."

"Did he frighten you?"

"Yes, he frightened me very much for some reason."

"Did you talk to him about us?"

"Yes. Oh, yes, I told him all about us and about Gipsy's Acre and about the house. He told me then that we'd have to take a chance with him. He's a very ill man. He said he thought he still had the life left in him to go and see the site, to draw the plans, to visualize it, and get it all sketched out. He said he wouldn't mind really if he died before the house was finished, but I told him," added Ellie, "that he mustn't die before the house was finished because I wanted him to see us live in it."

"What did he say to that?"

"He asked me if I knew what I was doing marrying you, and I said of course I did."

"And then?"

"He said he wondered if you knew what you were doing."

"I know, all right," I said.

"He said, 'You will always know where you're going,

44

Miss Guteman.' He said, 'You'll be going always where you want to go and because it's your chosen way.'

" 'But Mike,' he said, 'might take the wrong road. He hasn't grown up enough yet to know where he's going.'

"I said," said Ellie, " 'he'll be quite safe with me.' "

She had superb self-confidence. I was angry, though, at what Santonix had said. He was like my mother. She always seemed to know more about me than I knew myself.

"I know where I'm going," I said. "I'm going the way I want to go and we're going it together."

"They've started pulling down the ruins of The Towers already," said Ellie.

She began to talk practically.

"It's to be a rush job as soon as the plans are finished. We must hurry. Santonix said so. Shall we be married next Tuesday?" said Ellie. "It's a nice day of the week."

"With nobody else there," I said.

"Except Greta," said Ellie.

"To hell with Greta," I said. "She's not coming to our wedding. You and I and nobody else. We can pull the necessary witnesses out of the street."

I really think, looking back, that that was the happiest day of my life. . . .

BOOK TWO

9

So that was that, and Ellie and I got married. It sounds abrupt just putting it like that, but you see it was really just the way things happened. We decided to be married, and we got married.

It was part of the whole thing—not just an end to a romantic novel or a fairy story. "And so they got married and lived happily ever afterward." You can't, after all, make a big drama out of living happily ever afterward. We were married and we were both happy and it was really quite a time before anyone got on to us and began to make the usual difficulties and commotions, and we'd made up our mind to those.

The whole thing was really extraordinarily simple. In her desire for freedom Ellie had covered her tracks very cleverly up to now. The useful Greta had taken all the necessary steps and was always on guard behind her. And I had realized fairly soon that there was nobody really whose business it was to care terribly about Ellie and what she was doing. She had a stepmother who was engrossed in her own social life and love affairs. If Ellie didn't wish to accompany her to any particular spot on the globe, there was no need for Ellie to do so. She'd had all the proper governesses and lady's maids and scholastic advantages, and if she wanted to go to Europe, why not? If she chose to have her twenty-first birthday in London, again why not? Now that she had come into her vast fortune, she had the whip hand of her family in so far as spending her money went. If she wanted a villa on the Riviera or a castle on the Costa Brava or a yacht or any of those things, she had only to mention the fact and someone among the retinues that surround millionaires would put everything in hand immediately.

Greta, I gather, was regarded by her family as an admirable stooge. Competent, able to make all arrangements with the utmost efficiency, subservient, no doubt, and charming to the stepmother, the uncle and a few odd cousins who seemed to be knocking about. Ellie had no fewer than three lawyers at her command, from what she let fall every now and then. She was surrounded by a vast financial network of bankers and lawyers and the administrators of trust funds. It was a world that I just got glimpses of every now and then, mostly from things that Ellie let fall carelessly in the course of conversation. It didn't occur to her, naturally, that I wouldn't know about all those things. She had been brought up in the midst of them and she naturally concluded that the whole world knew what they were and how they worked and all the rest of it.

In fact, getting glimpses of the special peculiarities of each other's lives was unexpectedly what we enjoyed most in our early married life. To put it quite crudely—and I did put things crudely to myself, for that was the only way to get to terms with my new life—the poor don't really know how the rich live, and the rich don't know how the poor live, and to find out is really enchanting to both of them. Once I said uneasily,

"Look here, Ellie. Is there going to be an awful schemozzle over all this, over our marriage, I mean?"

Ellie considered without, I noticed, very much interest.

"Oh, yes," she said, "they'll probably be awful." And she added, "I hope you won't mind too much."

"I won't mind—why should I?—but you. Will they bully you over it?"

"I expect so," said Ellie, "but one needn't listen. The point is that they can't do anything."

"But they'll try?"

"Oh, yes," said Ellie. "They'll try." Then she added thoughtfully, "They'll probably try and buy you off."

"Buy me off?"

"Don't look so shocked," said Ellie, and she smiled a rather happy little girl's smile. "It isn't put exactly like that." Then she added, "They bought off Minnie Thompson's first, you know."

"Minnie Thompson? Is that the one they always call the oil heiress?"

"Yes, that's right. She ran off and married a life guard off the beach."

"Look here, Ellie," I said uneasily. "I was a life guard at Littlehampton once."

"Oh, were you? What fun! Permanently?"

"No, of course not. Just one summer, that's all."

"I wish you wouldn't worry," said Ellie.

"What happened about Minnie Thompson?"

"They had to go up to two hundred thousand dollars, I think," said Ellie. "He wouldn't take less. Minnie was man-mad and really a half-wit," she added.

"You take my breath away, Ellie," I said. "I've not only acquired a wife. I've got something I can trade for solid cash at any time."

"That's right," said Ellie. "Send for a high-powered lawyer and tell him you're willing to talk turkey. Then he fixes up the divorce and the amount of alimony," said Ellie, continuing my education. "My stepmother's been married four times," she added, "and she's made quite a lot out of it." And then she said, "Oh, Mike, don't look so shocked."

The funny thing is that I was shocked. I felt a priggish distaste for the corruption of modern society in its richer phases. There had been something so little-girl-like about Ellie, so simple, almost touching in her attitude, that I was astonished to find how well up she was in worldly

48

affairs and how much she took for granted. And yet I knew that I was right about her fundamentally. I knew quite well the kind of creature that Ellie was. Her simplicity, her affection, her natural sweetness. That didn't mean she had to be ignorant of things. What she did know and took for granted was a fairly limited slice of humanity. She didn't know much about my world, the world of scrounging for jobs, of race course gangs and dope gangs, the rough-and-tumble dangers of life, the sharp-aleck flashy type that I knew so well from living among them all my life. She didn't know what it was to be brought up decent and respectable but always hard up for money, with a mother who worked her fingers to the bone in the name of respectability, determining that her son should do well in life. Every penny scrimped for and saved, and the bitterness when your gay carefree son threw away his chances or gambled his all on a good tip.

She enjoyed hearing about my life as much as I enjoyed hearing about hers. Both of us were exploring a foreign country.

Looking back, I see what a wonderfully happy life it was, those early days with Ellie. At the time I took them for granted, and so did she. We were married in a registry office in Plymouth. Guteman is not an uncommon name. Nobody, reporters or otherwise, knew the Guteman heiress was in England. There had been vague paragraphs in papers occasionally, describing her as in Italy or on someone's yacht. We were married in the registrar's office, with his clerk and a middle-aged typist as witnesses. He gave us a serious little harangue on the serious responsibilities of married life, and wished us happiness. Then we went out, free and married. Mr. and Mrs. Michael Rogers! We spent a week in a seaside hotel and then we went abroad. We had a glorious three weeks traveling about wherever the fancy took us and no expense spared.

We went to Greece, and we went to Florence, and to Venice and lay on the Lido, then to the French Riviera and then to the Dolomites. Half the places I forget the names of now. We took planes or chartered a yacht or hired large and handsome cars. And while we enjoyed ourselves, Greta, I gathered from Ellie, was still on the home front doing her stuff.

Traveling about in her own way, sending letters and forwarding all the various post cards and letters that Ellie had left with her.

"There'll be a day of reckoning, of course," said Ellie. "They'll come down on us like a cloud of vultures. But we might as well enjoy ourselves until that happens."

"What about Greta?" I said. "Won't they be rather angry with her when they find out?"

"Oh, of course," said Ellie, "but Greta won't mind. She's tough."

"Mightn't it stop her getting another job?"

"Why should she get another job?" said Ellie. "She'll come and live with us."

"No!" I said.

"What do you mean, no, Mike?"

"We don't want anyone living with us," I said.

"Greta wouldn't be in the way," said Ellie, "and she'd be very useful. Really, I don't know what I'd do without her. I mean, she manages and arranges everything."

I frowned. "I don't think I'd like that. Besides, we want our own house—our dream house. After all, Ellie—we want it to ourselves."

"Yes," said Ellie, "I know what you mean. But all the same—" She hesitated. "I mean, it would be very hard on Greta not to have anywhere to live. After all, she's been with me, done everything for me for four years now. And look how she's helped me to get married and all that."

"I won't have her butting in between us all the time!"

"But she's not like that at all, Mike. You haven't even met her yet."

"No. No, I know I haven't, but—but it's nothing to do with, oh, with liking her or not. We want to be by ourselves, Ellie."

"Darling Mike," said Ellie softly.

We left it at that for the moment.

During the course of our travels we had met Santonix. That was in Greece. He had been in a small fisherman's cottage near the sea. I was startled by how ill he looked, much worse than when I had seen him a year ago. He greeted both Ellie and myself very warmly.

"So you've done it, you two," he said.

"Yes," said Ellie, "and now we're going to have our house built, aren't we?"

"I've got the drawings for you here, the plans," he said to me. "She's told you, hasn't she, how she came and ferreted me out and gave me her—commands," he said, choosing the word thoughtfully.

"Oh! not commands," said Ellie. "I just pleaded."

"You know we've bought the site?" I said.

"Ellie wired and told me. She sent me dozens of photographs."

"Of course you've got to come and see it first," said Ellie. "You mightn't like the site."

"I do like it."

"You can't really know till you've seen it."

"But I have seen it, child. I flew over five days ago. I met one of your hatchet-faced lawyers there—the English one."

"Mr. Crawford?"

"That's the man. In fact, operations have already started: clearing the ground, removing the ruins of the old house, foundations—drains— When you get back to England, I'll be there to meet you." He got out his plans then and we sat talking and looking at our house-to-be. There was even a rough water-color sketch of it as well as the architectural elevations and plans.

"Do you like it, Mike?"

I drew a deep breath.

"Yes," I said, "that's it. That's absolutely it."

"You used to talk about it enough, Mike. When I was in a fanciful mood, I used to think that piece of land had laid a spell upon you. You were a man in love with a house that you might never own, that you might never see, that might never even be built.

"But it's going to be built," said Ellie. "It's going to be built, isn't it?"

"If God or the devil wills it," said Santonix. "It doesn't depend on me."

"You're not any—any better?" I asked doubtfully.

"Get it into your thick head. I shall never be better. That's not on the cards."

"Nonsense," I said. "People are finding cures for things all the time. Doctors are gloomy brutes. They give people up for dead, and then the people laugh and cock a snook at them and live for another fifty years."

"I admire your optimism, Mike, but my malady isn't one of that kind. They take you to a hospital and give you a change of blood and back you come again with a little leeway of life, a little span of time gained. And so on, getting weaker each time."

"You are very brave," said Ellie.

"Oh, no, I'm not brave. When a thing is certain, there's nothing to be brave about. All you can do is to find your consolation."

"Building houses?"

"No, not that. You've less vitality all the time, you see, and therefore building houses becomes more difficult, not easier. The strength keeps giving out. No. But there are consolations. Sometimes very queer ones."

"I don't understand you," I said.

"No, you wouldn't, Mike. I don't know really that Ellie would. She might." He went on, speaking not so much to us as to himself. "Two things run together, side by side. Weakness and strength. The weakness of fading vitality and the strength of frustrated power. It doesn't matter, you see, what you do now! You're going to die anyway. So you can do anything you choose. There's nothing to deter you; there's nothing to hold you back. I could walk through the streets of Athens shooting down every man or woman whose face I didn't like. Think of that."

"The police could arrest you just the same," I pointed out.

"Of course they could. But what could they do? At the most take my life. Well, my life's going to be taken by a greater power than the law in a very short time. What else could they do? Send me to prison for twenty—thirty years? That's rather ironical, isn't it? There aren't twenty or thirty years for me to serve. Six months—one year—

eighteen months at the utmost. There's nothing anyone can do to me. So in the span that's left to me I am king. I can do what I like. Sometimes it's a very heady thought. Only—only, you see, there's not much temptation because there's nothing particularly exotic or lawless that I want to do."

After we had left him, as we were driving back to Athens, Ellie said to me,

"He's an odd person. Sometimes, you know, I feel frightened of him."

"Frightened of Rudolf Santonix—why?"

"Because he isn't like other people and because he has a—I don't know—a ruthlessness and an arrogance about him somewhere. And I think that he was trying to tell us, really, that knowing he's going to die soon has increased his arrogance. Supposing," said Ellie, looking at me, in an animated way, with almost a rapt and emotional expression on her face, "supposing he built us a lovely castle, our lovely house on the cliff's edge there in the pines, supposing we were coming to live in it. There he was on the doorstep and he welcomed us in and then—"

"Well, Ellie?"

"Then, supposing he came in after us, he slowly closed the doorway behind us, and sacrificed us there on the threshold. Cut our throats or something."

"You frighten me, Ellie. The things you think of!"

"The trouble with you and me, Mike, is that we don't live in the real world. We dream of fantastic things that may never happen."

"Don't think of sacrifices in connection with Gipsy's Acre."

"It's the name, I suppose, and the curse upon it."

"There isn't any curse," I shouted. "It's all nonsense. Forget it."

That was in Greece.

10

It was, I think, the day after that. We were in Athens. Suddenly, on the steps of the Acropolis, Ellie ran into people that she knew. They had come ashore from one of the Hellenic cruises. A woman of about thirty-five detached herself from the group and rushed along the steps to Ellie exclaiming,

"Why, I never did. It's really you, Ellie Guteman? Well, what are you doing here? I'd no idea. Are you on a cruise?"

"No," said Ellie, "just staying here."

"My, but it's lovely to see you. How's Cora? Is she here?"

"No, Cora is at Salzburg, I believe."

"Well, well." The woman was looking at me and Ellie said quietly, "Let me introduce—Mr. Rogers, Mrs. Bennington."

"How d'you do. How long are you here for?"

"I'm leaving tomorrow," said Ellie.

"Oh, dear! My, I'll lose my party if I don't go, and I just don't want to miss a word of the lecture and the descriptions. They do hustle one a bit, you know. I'm just beat at the end of the day. Any chance of meeting you for a drink?"

"Not today," said Ellie; "we're going on an excursion."

Mrs. Bennington rushed off to rejoin her party. Ellie, who had been going with me up the steps of the Acropolis, turned round and moved down again.

"That rather settles things, doesn't it?" she said to me.

"What does it settle?"

Ellie did not answer for a minute or two and then she said with a sigh, "I must write tonight."

"Write to whom?"

"Oh, to Cora, and to Uncle Frank, I suppose, and Uncle Andrew."

"Who's Uncle Andrew? He's a new one."

"Andrew Lippincott. Not really an uncle. He's my principal guardian or trustee or whatever you call it. He's a lawyer—a very well-known one."

"What are you going to say?"

"I'm going to tell them I'm married. I couldn't say suddenly to Nora Bennington, 'Let me introduce my husband.' There would have been frightful shrieks and exclamations and 'I never heard you were married. Tell me all about it, darling,' et cetera, et cetera, et cetera. It's only fair that my stepmother and Uncle Frank and Uncle Andrew should be the first to know." She sighed. "Oh, well, we've had a lovely time up to now."

"What will they all say or do?" I asked.

"Make a fuss, I expect," said Ellie in her placid way. "It doesn't matter if they do, and they'll have sense enough to know that. We'll have to have a meeting, I expect. We could go to New York. Would you like that?" She looked at me inquiringly.

"No," I said, "I shouldn't like it in the least."

"Then they'll come to London, probably, or some of them will. I don't know if you'd like that any better."

"I shouldn't like any of it. I want to be with you and see our house going up brick by brick as soon as Santonix gets there."

"So we can," said Ellie. "After all, meetings with the family won't take long. Possibly just one big splendid row would do. Get it over in one. Either we fly over there or they fly over here."

"I thought you said your stepmother was at Salzburg."

"Oh, I just said that. It sounded odd to say I didn't know where she was. Yes," said Ellie with a sigh, "we'll go home and meet them all. Mike, I hope you won't mind too much."

"Mind what—your family?"

"Yes. You won't mind if they're nasty to you?"

"I suppose it's the price I have to pay for marrying you," I said. "I'll bear it."

"There's your mother," said Ellie thoughtfully.

"For heaven's sake, Ellie, you're not going to try and arrange a meeting between your stepmother in her frills and her furbelows and my mother from her back street. What do you think they'd ever have to say to each other?"

"If Cora was my own mother they might have quite a lot to say to each other," said Ellie. "I wish you wouldn't be so obsessed with class distinctions, Mike!"

"Me!" I said incredulously. "What's your American phrase—I come from the wrong side of the tracks, don't I?"

"You don't want to write it on a placard and pin it on yourself."

"I don't know the right clothes to wear," I said bitterly. "I don't know the right way to talk about things and I don't know anything really about pictures or art or music. I'm only just learning who to tip and how much to give."

"Don't you think, Mike, that that makes it all much more exciting for you? I think so."

"Anyway," I said, "you're not to drag my mother into your family party."

"I wasn't proposing to drag anyone into anything, but I think, Mike, I ought to go and see your mother when we go back to England."

"No," I said explosively.

She looked at me rather startled.

"Why not, Mike, though? I mean, apart from anything else, I mean it's just very rude not to. Have you told her you're married?"

"Not yet."

"Why not?"

I didn't answer.

"Wouldn't the simplest way be to tell her you're married and take me to see her when we get back to England?"

"No," I said again. It was not so explosive this time but it was still fairly well underlined.

"You don't want me to meet her," said Ellie slowly.

I didn't, of course. I suppose it was obvious enough, but the last thing I could do was to explain. I didn't see how I could explain.

"It wouldn't be the right thing to do," I said slowly. "You must see that. I'm sure it would lead to trouble."

"You think she wouldn't like me?"

"Nobody could help liking you, but it wouldn't be— Oh, I don't know how to put it. But she might be upset and confused. After all, well, I mean I've married out of my station. That's the old-fashioned term. She wouldn't like that."

Ellie shook her head slowly.

"Does anybody really think like that nowadays?"

"Of course they do. They do in your country, too."

"Yes," she said, "in a way that's true, but—if anyone makes good there—"

"You mean if a man makes a lot of money."

"Well, not only money."

"Yes," I said, "it's money. If a man makes a lot of money, he's admired and looked up to and it doesn't matter where he was born."

"Well, that's the same everywhere," said Ellie.

"Please, Ellie," I said. "Please don't go and see my mother."

"I still think it's unkind."

"No, it isn't. Can't you let me know what's best for my own mother? She'd be upset. I tell you she would."

"But you must tell her you've got married."

"All right," I said. "I'll do that."

It occurred to me that it would be easier to write to my mother from abroad. That evening when Ellie was writing to Uncle Andrew and Uncle Frank and her stepmother Cora van Stuyvesant, I, too, was writing my own letter. It was quite short.

"Dear Mum," I wrote. "I ought to have told you before but I felt a bit awkward. I got married three weeks ago. It was all rather sudden. She's a very pretty girl and very sweet. She's got a lot of money, which makes things a bit awkward sometimes. We're going to build ourselves a house somewhere in the country. Just at present we're traveling around Europe. All the best. Yours, Mike."

The results of our evening's correspondence were somewhat varied. My mother let a week elapse before she sent a letter remarkably typical of her.

"Dear Mike. I was glad to get your letter. I hope you'll be very happy. Your affectionate mother."

As Ellie had prophesied, there was far more fuss on her side. We'd stirred up a regular hornet's nest of trouble. We were beset by reporters who wanted news of our romantic marriage, there were articles in the papers about the Guteman heiress and her romantic elopement, there were letters from bankers and lawyers. And finally official meetings were arranged. We met Santonix on the site of Gipsy's Acre and we looked at the plans there and discussed things, and then having seen things under way we came to London, took a suite at Claridge's and prepared, as they say in old-world books, to receive cavalry.

The first to arrive was Mr. Andrew P. Lippincott. He was an elderly man, dry and precise in appearance. He was long and lean, with suave and courteous manners. He was a Bostonian and from his voice I wouldn't have known he was an American. By arrangement through the telephone he called upon us in our suite at 12 o'clock. Ellie was nervous, I could tell, although she concealed it very well.

Mr. Lippincott kissed Ellie and extended a hand and a pleasant smile to me.

"Well, Ellie my dear, you are looking very well. Blooming, I might say."

"How are you, Uncle Andrew? How did you come? Did you fly?"

"No, I had a very pleasant trip across on the *Queen Mary*. And this is your husband?"

"This is Mike, yes."

I played up, or thought I did. "How are you, sir?" I said. Then I asked him if he'd have a drink, which he refused pleasantly. He sat down in an upright chair with gilt arms to it and looked, still smiling, from Ellie to me.

"Well," he said, "you young people have been giving us shocks. All very romantic, eh?"

"I'm sorry," said Ellie; "I really am sorry."

"Are you?" said Mr. Lippincott rather dryly.

"I thought it was the best way," said Ellie.

"I am not altogether of your opinion there, my dear."

"Uncle Andrew," Ellie said, "you know perfectly well that if I'd done it any other way, there would have been the most frightful fuss."

"Why should there have been such a frightful fuss?"

"You know what they'd have been like," said Ellie. "You, too," she added accusingly. She added, "I've had two letters from Cora. One yesterday and one this morning."

"You must discount a certain amount of agitation, my dear. It's only natural under the circumstances, don't you think?"

"It's my business who I get married to and how and where."

"You may think so, but you will find that the women of any family would rarely agree as to that."

"Really, I've saved everyone a lot of trouble."

"You may put it that way."

"But it's true, isn't it?"

"But you practiced, did you not, a good deal of deception, helped by someone who should have known better than to do what she did."

Ellie flushed.

"You mean Greta? She only did what I asked her to. Are they all very upset with her?"

"Naturally. Neither she nor you could expect anything else, could you? She was, remember, in a position of trust."

"I'm of age. I can do what I like."

"I am speaking of the period of time before you were of age. The deceptions began then, did they not?"

"You mustn't blame Ellie, sir," I said. "To begin with, I didn't know what was going on, and since all her relations are in another country, it wasn't easy for me to get in touch with them."

"I quite realize," said Mr. Lippincott, "that Greta posted certain letters and gave certain information to Mrs. Van Stuyvesant and to myself as she was requested to do by Ellie here, and made, if I may say so, a very competent job of it. You have met Greta Andersen, Michael? I may call you Michael, since you are Ellie's husband."

"Of course," I said, "call me Mike. No, I haven't met Miss Andersen——"

"Indeed? That seems to me surprising." He looked at me with a long thoughtful gaze. "I should have thought that she would have been present at your marriage."

"No, Greta wasn't there," said Ellie. She threw me a look of reproach and I shifted uncomfortably.

Mr. Lippincott's eyes were still resting on me thoughtfully. He made me uncomfortable. He seemed about to say something more, then changed his mind.

"I'm afraid," he said after a moment or two, "that you two, Michael and Ellie, will have to put up with a certain amount of reproaches and criticism from Ellie's family."

"I suppose they are going to descend on me in a bunch," said Ellie.

"Very probably," said Mr. Lippincott. "I've tried to pave the way," he added.

"You're on our side, Uncle Andrew?" said Ellie, smiling at him.

"You must hardly ask a prudent lawyer to go as far as that. I have learned that in life it is wise to accept what is a *fait accompli*. You two have fallen in love with each other and have got married and have, I understood you to say, Ellie, bought a piece of property in the south of England and are already starting building a house on it. You propose, therefore, to live in this country?"

"We want to make our home here, yes. Do you object to our doing that?" I said with a touch of anger in my voice. "Ellie's married to me and she's a British subject now. So why shouldn't she live in England?"

"No reason at all. In fact, there is no reason why Fenella should not live in any country she chooses, or indeed have property in more than one country. The house in Nassau belongs to you, remember, Ellie."

"I always thought it was Cora's. She always has behaved as though it was."

"But the actual property rights are vested in you. You also have the house in Long Island whenever you care to visit it. You are the owner of a great deal of oil-bearing property in the West." His voice was amiable, pleasant, but I had the feeling that the words were directed at me in some curious way. Was it his idea of trying to insinuate a wedge between me and Ellie? I was not sure. It didn't seem very sensible, rubbing it in to a man that his wife owned property all over the world and was fabulously rich. If anything, I should have thought that he would have played down Ellie's property rights and her money and all the rest of it. If I was a fortune hunter, as he obviously thought, that would be all the more grist to my mill. But I did realize that Mr. Lippincott was a subtle man. It would be hard at any time to know what he was driving at —what he had in his mind behind his even and pleasant manner. Was he trying in a way of his own to make me feel uncomfortable, to make me feel that I was going to be branded almost publicly as a fortune hunter? He said to Ellie,

"I've brought over a certain amount of legal stuff which you'll have to go through with me, Ellie. I shall want your signature to many of these things."

"Yes, of course, Uncle Andrew. Any time."

"As you say, any time. There's no hurry. I have other business in London, and I shall be over here for about ten days."

Ten days, I thought. That's a long time. I rather wished that Mr. Lippincott wasn't going to be here for ten days. He appeared friendly enough toward me, though, as you might say, indicating that he still reserved his judgment on certain points, but I wondered at that moment whether he was really my enemy. If he was, he would not be the kind of man to show his hand.

"Well," he went on, "now that we've all met and come to terms, as you might say, for the future, I would like to have a short interview with this husband of yours."

Ellie said, "You can talk to us both." She was up in arms. I put a hand on her arm.

"Now don't flare up, ducks; you're not a mother hen protecting a chicken." I propelled her gently to the door in the wall that led into the bedroom. "Uncle Andrew wants to size me up," I said. "He's well within his rights."

I pushed her gently through the double doors. I shut them both and came back into the room. It was a large, handsome sitting room. I came back and took a chair and faced Mr. Lippincott. "All right," I said. "Shoot."

"Thank you, Michael," he said. "First of all I want to assure you that I am not, as you may be thinking, your enemy in any way."

"Well," I said, "I'm glad to hear that." I didn't sound very sure about it.

"Let me speak frankly," said Mr. Lippincott, "more frankly than I could do before that dear child to whom I am guardian and of whom I am very fond. You may not yet appreciate it fully, Michael, but Ellie is a most unusually sweet and lovable girl."

"Don't you worry. I'm in love with her, all right."

"That is not at all the same thing," said Mr. Lippincott in his dry manner. "I hope that as well as being in love with her you can also appreciate what a really dear and in some ways very vulnerable person she is."

"I'll try," I said. "I don't think I'll have to try very hard. She's tops, Ellie is."

"So I will go on with what I was about to say. I shall put my cards on the table with the utmost frankness. You are not the kind of young man that I should have wished Ellie to marry. I should like her, as her family would have liked her, to marry someone of her own surroundings, of her own set—"

"A toff, in other words," I said.

"No, not only that. A similar background is, I think, to be desired as a basis for matrimony. And I am not referring to the snob attitude. After all, Herman Guteman, her grandfather, started life as a dock hand. He ended up as one of the richest men in America."

"For all you know I might do the same," I said. "I may end up one of the richest men in England."

"Everything is possible," said Mr. Lippincott. "Do you have ambitions that way?"

"It's not just the money," I said. "I'd like to—I'd like

to get somewhere and do things and—" I hesitated, stopped.

"You have ambitions, shall we say? Well, that is a very good thing, I am sure."

"I'm starting at long odds," I said, "starting from scratch. I'm nothing and nobody and I won't pretend otherwise."

He nodded approval.

"Very frankly and handsomely said. I appreciate it. Now, Michael, I am no relation to Ellie, but I have acted as her guardian, I am a trustee, left so by her grandfather, of her affairs, I manage her fortune and her investments. And I assume, therefore, a certain responsibility for them. Therefore I want to know all that I can know about the husband she has chosen."

"Well," I said, "you can make inquiries about me, I suppose, and find out anything you like easily enough."

"Quite so," said Mr. Lippincott. "That would be one way of doing it. A wise precaution to take. But actually, Michael, I should like to know all that I can about you from your own lips. I should like to hear your own story of what your life has been up to now."

Of course I didn't like it. I expect he knew I wouldn't. Nobody in my position would like that. It's second nature to make the best of yourself. I'd made a point of that at school and onward, boasted about things a bit, said a few things, stretching the truth a bit. I wasn't ashamed of it. I think it's natural. I think it's the sort of thing that you've got to do if you want to get on. Make out a good case for yourself. People take you at your own valuation, and I didn't want to be like that chap in Dickens. They read it out on the television, and I must say it's a good yarn on its own. Uriah something his name was, always going about being humble and rubbing his hands, and actually planning and scheming behind that humility. I didn't want to be like that.

I was ready enough to boast a bit with the chaps I met or to put up a good case to a prospective employer. After all, you've got a best side and a worst side of yourself and it's no good showing the worst side and harping on it. No,

I'd always done the best for myself describing my activities up to date. But I didn't fancy doing that sort of thing with Mr. Lippincott. He'd rather pooh-poohed the idea of making private inquiries about me, but I wasn't at all sure that he wouldn't do so, all the same. So I gave him the truth unvarnished, as you might say.

Squalid beginnings, the fact that my father had been a drunk, but that I'd had a good mother, that she'd slaved a good bit to help me get educated. I made no secret of the fact that I'd been a rolling stone, that I'd moved from one job to another. He was a good listener, encouraging, if you know what I mean. Every now and then, though, I realized how shrewd he was. Just little questions that he slipped in, or comments, some comment that I might have rushed in unguardedly either to admit or to deny.

Yes, I had a sort of feeling that I'd better be wary and on my toes. And after ten minutes I was quite glad when he leaned back in his chair and the inquisition, if you could call it that, and it wasn't in the least like one, seemed to be over.

"You have an adventurous attitude to life, Mr. Rogers —Michael. Not a bad thing. Tell me more about this house that you and Ellie are building."

"Well," I said, "it's not far from a town called Market Chadwell."

"Yes," he said, "I know just where it is. As a matter of fact, I ran down to see it. Yesterday, to be exact."

That startled me a little. It showed he was a devious kind of fellow who got round to more things than you might think he would.

"It's a beautiful site," I said defensively, "and the house we're building is going to be a beautiful house. The architect's a chap called Santonix—Rudolf Santonix. I don't know if you've ever heard of him, but—"

"Oh, yes," said Mr. Lippincott, "he's quite a well-known name among architects."

"He's done work in the States, I believe."

"Yes, an architect of great promise and talent. Unfortunately I believe his health is not good."

"He thinks he's a dying man," I said, "but I don't be-

64

lieve it. I believe he'll get cured, get well again. Doctors—they'll say anything."

"I hope your optimism is justified. You are an optimist."

"I am about Santonix."

"I hope all you wish will come true. I may say that I think you and Ellie have made an extremely good purchase in the piece of property that you have bought."

I thought it was nice of the old boy to use the pronoun "you." It wasn't rubbing it in that Ellie had done the buying on her own.

"I have had a consultation with Mr. Crawford—"

"Crawford?" I frowned slightly.

"Mr. Crawford of Reece and Crawford, a firm of English solicitors. Mr. Crawford was the member of the firm who put the purchase in hand. It is a good firm of solicitors and I gather that this property was acquired at a cheap figure. I may say that I wondered slightly at that. I am familiar with the present prices of land in this country and I really felt rather at a loss to account for it. I think Mr. Crawford himself was surprised to get it at so low a figure. I wondered if you knew at all why this property happened to go so cheaply. Mr. Crawford did not advance any opinion on that. In fact he seemed slightly embarrassed when I put the question to him."

"Oh, well," I said, "it's got a curse on it."

"I beg your pardon, Michael. What did you say?"

"A curse, sir," I explained. "The gipsy's warning, that sort of thing. It is known locally as Gipsy's Acre."

"Ah. A story?"

"Yes. It seems rather confused and I don't know how much people have made up and how much is true. There was a murder or something long ago. A man and his wife and another man. Some story that the husband shot the other two and then shot himself. At least that's the verdict that was brought in. But all sorts of other stories go flying about. I don't think anyone really knows what happened. It was a good long time ago. It's changed hands about four or five times since, but nobody stays there long."

"Ah," said Mr. Lippincott appreciatively, "yes, quite a

piece of English folklore." He looked at me curiously. "And you and Ellie are not afraid of the curse?" He said it lightly, with a slight smile.

"Of course not," I said. "Neither Ellie nor I would believe in any rubbish of that kind. Actually, it's a lucky thing, since because of it we got it cheap." When I said that, a sudden thought struck me. It was lucky in one sense, but I thought that with all Ellie's money and her property and all the rest of it, it couldn't matter to her very much whether she bought a piece of land cheap or at the top price. Then I thought, no, I was wrong. After all, she'd had a grandfather who came up from being a dock laborer to a millionaire. Anyone of that kind would always wish to buy cheap and sell dear.

"Well, I am not superstitious," said Mr. Lippincott, "and the view from your property is quite magnificent." He hesitated. "I only hope that when you come to move into your house to live there, that Ellie will not hear too many of these stories that are going about."

"I'll keep everything from her that I can," I said. "I don't suppose anybody will say anything to her."

"People in country villages are very fond of repeating stories of that kind," said Mr. Lippincott. "And Ellie, remember, is not as tough as you are, Michael. She can be influenced easily. Only in some ways. Which brings me—" he stopped without going on to say what he had been going to. He tapped on the table with one finger. "I'm going to speak to you now on a matter of some difficulty. You said just now that you had not met this Greta Andersen."

"No, as I said, I haven't met her yet."

"Odd. Very curious."

"Well?" I looked at him inquiringly.

"I should have thought you'd have been almost sure to have met her," he said slowly. "How much do you know about her?"

"I know that she's been with Ellie some time."

"She has been with Ellie since Ellie was seventeen. She has occupied a post of some responsibility and trust. She came first to the States in the capacity of secretary and companion. A kind of chaperon to Ellie when Mrs. Van

Stuyvesant, her stepmother, was away from home, which I may say was a quite frequent occurrence." He spoke particularly dryly when he said this. "She is, I gather, a well-born girl with excellent references, half Swedish, half German. Ellie became, quite naturally, very much attached to her."

"So I gather," I said.

"In some ways Ellie was, I suppose, almost too much attached to her. You don't mind my saying that."

"No. Why should I mind? As a matter of fact, I've—well, I've thought so myself once or twice. Greta this and Greta that. I got—well, I know I've no business to, but I used to get fed-up sometimes."

"And yet she expressed no wish for you to meet Greta?"

"Well," I said, "it's rather difficult to explain. But I think, yes, I think she probably did suggest it in a mild way once or twice but, well, we were too taken up with having met each other. Besides, oh, well, I suppose I didn't really want to meet Greta. I didn't want to share Ellie with anyone."

"I see. Yes, I see. And Ellie did not suggest Greta being present at your wedding?"

"She did suggest it," I said.

"But—but you didn't want her to come. Why?"

"I don't know. I really don't know. I just felt that this Greta, this girl or woman I'd never met, she was always horning in on everything. You know, arranging Ellie's life for her. Sending post cards and letters and filling in for Ellie, arranging a whole itinerary and passing it on to the family. I felt that Ellie was dependent on Greta in a way, that she let Greta run her, that she wanted to do everything that Greta wanted. I—oh, I'm sorry, Mr. Lippincott, I oughtn't to be saying all these things perhaps. Say I was just plain jealous. Anyway, I blew up and I said I didn't want Greta at the wedding, that the wedding was ours, that it was just our business and nobody else's. And so we went along to the registrar's office and his clerk and the typist from his office were the two witnesses. I daresay it was mean of me to refuse to have Greta there, but I wanted to have Ellie to myself."

"I see. Yes, I see, and I think, if I may say so, that you were wise, Michael."

"You don't like Greta either," I said shrewdly.

"You can hardly use the word 'either,' Michael, if you have not even met her."

"No, I know but, well, I mean if you hear a lot about a person, you can form some sort of idea of them, some judgment of them. Oh, well, call it plain jealousy. Why don't *you* like Greta?"

"This is without prejudice," said Mr. Lippincott, "but you are Ellie's husband, Michael, and I have Ellie's happiness very much at heart. I don't think that the influence that Greta has over Ellie is a very desirable one. She takes too much upon herself."

"Do you think she'll try and make trouble between us?" I asked.

"I think," said Mr. Lippincott, "that I have no right to say anything of that kind."

He sat looking cautiously at me and blinking like a wrinkled old tortoise.

I didn't know quite what to say next. He spoke first, choosing his words with some care.

"There has been, then, no suggestion that Greta Andersen might take up her residence with you?"

"Not if I can help it," I said.

"Ah. So that is what you feel? The idea has been mooted."

"Ellie did say something of the kind. But we're newly married, Mr. Lippincott. We want our house—our new home—to ourselves. Of course she'll come and stay sometimes, I suppose. That'll only be natural."

"As you say, that would be only natural. But you realize, perhaps, that Greta is going to be in a somewhat difficult position as regards further employment. I mean, it is not a question of what Ellie thinks of her, but of what the people who engaged her and reposed trust in her feel."

"You mean that you or Mrs. Van What's-her-name won't recommend her for another post of the same kind?"

"They are hardly likely to do so except so far as to satisfy purely legal requirements."

"And you think that she'll want to come to England and live on Ellie."

"I don't want to prejudice you too much against her. After all, this is mostly in my mind. I dislike some of the things she has done and the way she has done them. I think that Ellie, who has a very generous heart, will be upset at having, shall we say, blighted Greta's prospects in many ways. She might impulsively insist on her coming to live with you."

"I don't think Ellie will insist," I said slowly. I sounded a little worried all the same, and I thought Lippincott noticed it. "But couldn't we—Ellie, I mean—couldn't Ellie pension her off?"

"We should not put it precisely like that," said Mr. Lippincott. "There is a suggestion of age about pensioning anyone off, and Greta is a young woman, and I may say a very handsome young woman. Beautiful, in fact," he added in a deprecating, disapproving voice. "She's very attractive to men, too."

"Well, perhaps she'll marry," I said. "If she's all that, why hasn't she got married before this?"

"There have been people attracted, I believe, but she has not considered them. I think, however, that your suggestion is a very sound one. I think it might be carried out in a way that would not hurt anyone's susceptibilities. It might seem quite a natural thing to do on Ellie's having attained her majority and having had her marriage helped on by Greta's good offices—settle a sum of money upon her in a fit of gratitude." Mr. Lippincott made the last two words sound as sour as lemon juice.

"Well, then, that's all right," I said cheerfully.

"Again I see that you are an optimist. Let us hope that Greta will accept what is offered to her."

"Why shouldn't she? She'd be mad if she didn't."

"I don't know," said Mr. Lippincott. "I should say it would be extraordinary if she did not accept, and they will remain on terms of friendship, of course."

"You think— What do you think?"

"I would like to see her influence over Ellie broken," said Mr. Lippincott. He got up. "You will, I hope, assist me and do everything you can to further that end?"

"You bet I will," I said. "The last thing I want is to have Greta in our pockets all the time."

"You might change your mind when you see her," said Mr. Lippincott.

"I don't think so," I said. "I don't like managing females, however efficient and even handsome they are."

"Thank you, Michael, for listening to me so patiently. I hope you will give me the pleasure of dining with me, both of you. Possibly next Tuesday evening? Cora van Stuyvesant and Frank Barton will probably be in London by that time."

"And I've got to meet them, I suppose?"

"Oh, yes, that will be quite inevitable." He smiled at me and this time his smile seemed more genuine than it had before. "You mustn't mind too much," he said. "Cora, I expect, will be very rude to you. Frank will be merely tactless. Reuben won't be over just at present."

I didn't know who Reuben was—another relation, I supposed.

I went across to the connecting doors and opened them. "Come on, Ellie," I said, "the grilling is over."

She came back in the room and looked quickly from Lippincott to myself, then she went across and kissed him.

"Dear Uncle Andrew," she said. "I can see you've been nice to Michael."

"Well, my dear, if I weren't nice to your husband, you wouldn't have much use for me in the future, would you? I do reserve the right to give a few words of advice now and then. You're very young, you know, both of you."

"All right," said Ellie, "we'll listen patiently."

"Now, my dear, I'd like to have a word with you if I may."

"My turn to be odd man out," I said, and I too went into the bedroom.

I shut the two double doors ostentatiously, but I opened the inner one again after I got inside. I hadn't been as well brought up as Ellie, so I felt a bit anxious to find out how double-faced Mr. Lippincott might turn out to be. But actually there was nothing I need have listened to. He gave Ellie one or two wise words of advice. He said she must realize that I might find it difficult to be a poor man married to a rich wife, and then he went on to sound her about making a settlement on Greta. She agreed to it eagerly and said she'd been going to ask him that herself. He also suggested that she should make an additional settlement on Cora van Stuyvesant.

"There is no earthly need that you should do so," he said. "She has been very well provided for in the matter of alimony from several husbands. And she is, as you know, paid an income, though not a very big one, from the trust fund left by your grandfather."

"But you think I ought to give her more still?"

"I think there is no legal or moral obligation to do so. What I think is that you will find her far less tiresome and shall I say catty if you do so. I should make it in the form of an increased income, which you could revoke at any time. If you find that she has been spreading malicious rumors about Michael or yourself or your life together, the knowledge that you can do that will keep her tongue free of those more poisonous barbs that she so well knows how to plant."

"Cora has always hated me," said Ellie. "I've known that." She added rather shyly, "You do like Mike, don't you, Uncle Andrew?"

"I think he's an extremely attractive young man," said Mr. Lippincott. "And I can quite see how you came to marry him."

That, I suppose, was as good as I could expect. I wasn't really his type, and I knew it. I eased the door gently to and in a minute or two Ellie came to fetch me.

We were both standing saying good-by to Lippincott when there was a knock on the door and a page boy came in with a telegram. Ellie took it and opened it. She gave a little surprised cry of pleasure.

"It's Greta," she said; "she's arriving in London tonight

and she'll be coming to see us tomorrow. How lovely."
She looked at us both. "Isn't it?" she said.

She saw two sour faces and heard two polite voices saying, one: "Yes, indeed, my dear," the other one: "Of course."

11

■

I had been out shopping the next morning and I arrived back at the hotel rather later than I had meant. I found Ellie sitting in the central lounge, and opposite her was a tall blonde young woman. In fact Greta. Both of them were talking nineteen to the dozen.

I'm never any hand at describing people, but I'll have a shot at describing Greta. To begin with, one couldn't deny that she was, as Ellie had said, very beautiful and also, as Mr. Lippincott had reluctantly admitted, very handsome. The two things are not exactly the same. If you say a woman is handsome, it does not mean that actually you yourself admire her. Mr. Lippincott, I gathered, had not admired Greta. All the same, when Greta walked across the lounge into a hotel or in a restaurant, men's heads turned to look at her. She was a Nordic type of blonde with pure gold corn-colored hair. She wore it piled high on her head in the fashion of the time, not falling straight down on each side of her face in the Chelsea tradition. She looked what she was—Swedish or north German. In fact, pin on a pair of wings and she could have gone to a fancy dress ball as a Valkyrie. Her eyes were a bright clear blue, and her contours were admirable. Let's admit it. She was something!

I came along to where they were sitting and joined them, greeting them both in what I hope was a natural, friendly manner, though I couldn't help feeling a bit awkward. I'm not always very good at acting a part. Ellie said immediately,

"At last, Mike, this is Greta."

I said I guessed it might be, in a rather facetious, not very happy manner. I said,

"I'm very glad to meet you at last, Greta."

Ellie said,

"As you know very well, if it hadn't been for Greta, we would never have been able to get married."

"All the same, we'd have managed it somehow," I said.

"Not if the family had come down on us like a ton of coals. They'd have broken it up somehow. Tell me, Greta, have they been very awful?" Ellie asked. "You haven't written or said anything to me about that."

"I know better," said Greta, "than to write to a happy couple when they're on their honeymoon."

"But were they very angry with you?"

"Of course! What do you imagine? But I was prepared for that, I can assure you."

"What have they said or done?"

"Everything they could," said Greta cheerfully. "Starting with the sack, naturally."

"Yes, I suppose that was inevitable. But—but what have you done? After all, they can't refuse to give you references."

"Of course they can. And after all, from their point of view I was placed in a position of trust and abused it shamefully." She added, "Enjoyed abusing it, too."

"But what are you doing now?"

"Oh, I've got a job ready to walk into."

"In New York?"

"No. Here in London. Secretarial."

"But are you all right?"

"Darling Ellie," said Greta, "how can I not be all right with that lovely check you sent me in anticipation of what was going to happen when the balloon went up."

Her English was very good, with hardly any trace of accent, though she used a lot of colloquial terms which sometimes didn't run quite right.

"I've seen a bit of the world, fixed myself up in London and bought a good many things as well."

"Mike and I have bought a lot of things, too," said Ellie, smiling at the recollection.

It was true. We'd done ourselves pretty well with our continental shopping. It was really wonderful that we had dollars to spend, no niggling treasury restrictions. Brocades and fabrics in Italy for the house. And we'd bought pictures, too, both in Italy and in Paris, paying what seemed fabulous sums for them. A whole world had opened up to me that I'd never dreamed would have come my way.

"You both look remarkably happy," said Greta.

"You haven't seen our house yet," said Ellie. "It's going to be wonderful. It's going to be just like we dreamed it would be, isn't it, Mike?"

"I have seen it," said Greta. "The first day I got back to England, I hired a car and drove down there."

"Well?" said Ellie.

I said Well? too.

"Well," said Greta consideringly. She shifted her head from side to side.

Ellie looked grief-stricken, horribly taken aback. But I wasn't taken in. I saw at once that Greta was having a bit of fun with us. If the thought just flashed across my mind for a moment that her kind of fun wasn't very kind, it hardly had time to take root. Greta burst out laughing, a high musical laugh that made people turn their heads and look at us.

"You should have seen your faces," she said, "especially yours, Ellie. I have to tease you just a little. It's a wonderful house, lovely. That man's a genius."

"Yes," I said, "he's something out of the ordinary. Wait till you meet him."

"I have met him," said Greta. "He was down there the day I went. Yes, he's an extraordinary person. Rather frightening, don't you think?"

"Frightening?" I said, surprised. "In what way?"

"Oh, I don't know. It's as though he looks through you and—well, sees right through to the other side. That's always disconcerting." Then she added, "He looks rather ill."

"He is ill. Very ill," I said.

"What a shame. What's the matter with him, tuberculosis, something like that?"

"No," I said, "I don't think it's tuberculosis. I think it's something to do with—oh, with blood."

"Oh, I see. Doctors can do almost anything nowadays, can't they, unless they kill you first while they're trying to cure you. But don't let's think of that. Let's think of the house. When will it be finished?"

"Quite soon, I should think, by the look of it. I'd never imagined a house could go up so quickly," I said.

"Oh," said Greta carelessly, "that's money. Double shifts and bonuses—all the rest of it. You don't really know yourself, Ellie, how wonderful it is to have all the money you have."

But I did know. I had been learning, learning a great deal in the last few weeks. I'd stepped as a result of marriage into an entirely different world, and it wasn't the sort of world I'd imagined it to be from the outside. So far in my life, a lucky double had been my highest knowledge of affluence. A whack of money coming in, and spending it as fast as I could on the biggest blow-out I could find. Crude, of course. The crudeness of my class. But Ellie's world was a different world. It wasn't what I should have thought it to be. Just more and more super luxury. It wasn't bigger bathrooms and larger houses and more electric light fittings and bigger meals and faster cars. It wasn't just spending for spending's sake and showing off to everyone in sight. Instead, it was curiously simple—the sort of simplicity that comes when you get beyond the point of splashing for splashing's sake. You don't want three yachts or four cars and you can't eat more than three meals a day, and if you buy a really top-price picture, you don't want more than perhaps one of them in a room. It's as simple as that. Whatever you have is just the best of its kind, not so much because it is the best but because there is no reason if you like or want any particular thing why you shouldn't have it. There is no moment when you say,

"I'm afraid I can't afford that one." So in a strange way it makes sometimes for such a curious simplicity that I couldn't understand it. We were considering a French impressionist picture, a Cézanne, I think it was. I had to learn that name carefully. I always mixed it up with a tzigane, which I gather is a gipsy orchestra. And then as we walked along the streets of Venice, Ellie stopped to look at some pavement artists. On the whole they were doing some terrible pictures for tourists which all looked the same. Portraits with great rows of shining teeth and usually blonde hair falling down their necks.

And then she bought quite a tiny picture, just a picture of a little glimpse through to a canal. The man who had painted it appraised the look of us and she bought it for £6 by English exchange. The funny thing was that I knew quite well that Ellie had just the same longing for that £6 picture that she had for the Cézanne.

It was the same way one day in Paris. She'd said to me suddenly,

"What fun it would be—let's get a really nice crisp French loaf of bread and have that with butter and one of those cheeses wrapped up in leaves."

So we did, and Ellie, I think, enjoyed it more than the meal we'd had the night before which had come to about £20 English. At first I couldn't understand it; then I began to see. The awkward thing was that I could see now that being married to Ellie wasn't just fun and games. You have to do your homework, you have to learn how to go into a restaurant and the sort of things to order and the right tips, and when for some reason you gave more than usual. You have to memorize what you drink with certain foods. I had to do most of it by observation. I couldn't ask Ellie because that was one of the things she wouldn't have understood. She'd have said, "But, darling Mike, you can have anything you like. What does it matter if waiters think you ought to have one particular wine with one particular thing?" It wouldn't have mattered to her because she was born to it, but it mattered to me because I couldn't do just as I liked. I wasn't simple enough. Clothes, too. Ellie was more helpful there, for she understood better. She just guided me to the right places and told me to let them have their head.

Of course I didn't look right and sound right yet. But that didn't matter much. I'd got the hang of it, enough so that I could pass muster with people like old Lippincott, and shortly, presumably, when Ellie's stepmother and uncles were around, but actually it wasn't going to matter in the future at all. When the house was finished and when we'd moved in, we were going to be far away from everybody. It could be our kingdom. I looked at Greta sitting opposite me. I wondered what she'd really thought of our house. Anyway, it was what I wanted. It satisfied me utterly. I wanted to drive down and go through a private path through the trees which led down to a small cove which would be our own beach which nobody could come to on the land side. It would be a thousand times better, I thought, plunging into the sea there. A thousand times better than a lido spread along a beach with hundreds of bodies lying there. I didn't want all the senseless rich things. I wanted—there were the words again, my own particular words—I want, I want . . . I could feel all the feeling surging up in me. I wanted a wonderful woman and a wonderful house like nobody else's house, and I wanted my wonderful house to be full of wonderful things—things that belonged to me. Everything would belong to me.

"He's thinking of our house," said Ellie.

It seemed that she had twice suggested to me that we should now go into the dining room. I looked at her affectionately.

Later in the day—it was that evening—when we were dressing to go out to dinner, Ellie said a little tentatively,

"Mike, you do—you do like Greta, don't you?"

"Of course I do," I said.

"I couldn't bear it if you didn't like her."

"But I do," I protested. "What makes you think I don't?"

"I'm not quite sure. I think it's the way you hardly look at her even when you're talking to her."

"Well, I suppose that's because—well, because I feel nervous."

"Nervous of Greta?"

"Yes, she's a bit awe-inspiring, you know."

And I told Ellie how I thought Greta looked rather like a Valkyrie.

"Not as stout as an operatic one," said Ellie, and laughed. We both laughed. I said,

"It's all very well for you because you've known her for years. But she is just a bit—well, I mean she's very efficient and practical and sophisticated." I struggled with a lot of words which didn't seem to be quite the right ones. I said suddenly, "I feel—I feel at a disadvantage with her."

"Oh, Mike!" Ellie was conscience-stricken. "I know we've got a lot of things to talk about. Old jokes and old things that happened and all that. I suppose—yes, I suppose it might make you feel rather shy. But you'll soon get to be friends. She likes you. She likes you very much. She told me so."

"Listen, Ellie, she'd probably tell you that anyway."

"Oh, no, she wouldn't. Greta's very outspoken. You heard her. Some of the things she said today."

It was true that Greta had not minced her words during luncheon. She had said, addressing me rather than Ellie,

"You must have thought it queer sometimes, the way I was backing Ellie up when I'd not even seen you. But I got so mad—so mad with the life that they were making her lead. All tied up in a cocoon with their money, their traditional ideas. She never had a chance to enjoy herself, go anywhere really by herself and do what she wanted. She wanted to rebel but she didn't know how. And so— yes, all right, I urged her on. I suggested she should look at properties in England. Then I said when she was twenty-one she could buy one of her own and say good-by to all that New York lot."

"Greta always has wonderful ideas," said Ellie. "She thinks of things I'd probably never have thought of myself."

What were those words Mr. Lippincott had said to me?

"She has too much influence over Ellie." I wondered if it was true. Queerly enough, I didn't really think so. I felt that there was a core somewhere in Ellie that Greta, for all that she knew her so well, had never quite appreciated. Ellie, I was sure, would always accept any ideas that matched with the ideas she wanted to have herself. Greta had preached rebellion to Ellie, but Ellie herself wanted to rebel, only she was not sure how to do so. But I felt that Ellie, now that I was coming to know her better, was one of those very simple people who have unexpected reserves. I thought Ellie would be quite capable of taking a stand of her own if she wished to. The point was that she wouldn't very often wish to, and I thought then how difficult everyone was to understand. Even Ellie. Even Greta. Even perhaps my own mother. . . . The way she looked at me with fear in her eyes.

I wondered about Mr. Lippincott. I said, as we were peeling some outsize peaches,

"Mr. Lippincott seems to have taken our marriage very well, really. I was surprised."

"Mr. Lippincott," said Greta, "is an old fox."

"You always say so, Greta," said Ellie, "but I think he's rather a dear. Very strict and proper and all that."

"Well, go on thinking so if you like," said Greta. "Myself, I wouldn't trust him an inch."

"Not trust him!" said Ellie.

Greta shook her head. "I know. He's a pillar of respectability and trustworthiness. He's everything a trustee and a lawyer should be."

Ellie laughed and said, "Do you mean he's embezzled my fortune? Don't be silly, Greta. There are thousands of auditors and banks and check-ups and all that sort of thing."

"Oh, I expect he's all right, really," said Greta. "All the same, those are the people that do embezzle. The trustworthy ones. And then everyone says afterwards, 'I'd never have believed it of Mr. A. or Mr. B. The last man in the world.' Yes, that's what they say. 'The last man in the world.'"

Ellie said thoughtfully that her Uncle Frank, she

thought, was much more likely to go in for dishonest practices. She did not seem unduly worried or surprised by the idea.

"Oh, well, he looks like a crook," said Greta. "That handicaps him to start with. All that geniality and bonhomie. But he'll never be in a position to be a crook in a big way."

"Is he your mother's brother or your father's brother?" I asked. I hadn't had time to think much about Ellie's relations.

"He's my father's sister's husband," said Ellie. "She left him and married someone else and died about six or seven years ago. Uncle Frank has more or less stuck on with the family."

"There are three of them," said Greta kindly and helpfully. "Three leeches hanging round, as you might say. Ellie's actual uncles were killed, one in Korea and one in a car accident, so what she's got is a much-damaged stepmother, an Uncle Frank, an amiable hanger-on in the family home, and her cousin Reuben who she calls uncle, but he's only a cousin, and Andrew Lippincott and Stanford Lloyd."

"Who is Stanford Lloyd?" I asked, bewildered.

"Oh, another sort of trustee, isn't he, Ellie? At any rate he manages your investments and things like that. Which can't be really very difficult, because when you've got as much money as Ellie has, it sort of makes more money all the time without her having to do much about it. Those are the main surrounding group," Greta added, "and I have no doubt that you will be meeting them fairly soon. They'll be over here to have a look at you."

I groaned and looked at Ellie. Ellie said very gently and sweetly,

"Never mind, Mike; they'll go away again."

12

They did come over. None of them stayed very long. Not that time—not on a first visit. They came over to have a look at me. I found them difficult to understand because, of course, they were all American. They were types with which I was not well acquainted. Some of them were pleasant enough. Uncle Frank, for instance. I agreed with Greta about him. I wouldn't have trusted him a yard. I had come across the same type in England. He was a big man with a bit of a paunch and pouches under his eyes that gave him a dissipated look which was not far from the truth, I imagine. He had an eye for women, I thought, and even more of an eye for the main chance. He borrowed money from me once or twice, quite small sums just, as it were, something to tide him over for a day or two. I thought it was not so much that he needed the money but he wanted to test me out, to see if I lent money easily. It was rather worrying because I wasn't sure which was the best way to take it. Would it have been better to refuse point-blank and let him know I was a skinflint or was it better to assume an appearance of careless generosity, which I was very far from feeling? To hell with Uncle Frank, I thought.

Cora, Ellie's stepmother, was the one that interested me most. She was a woman of about forty, well turned out, with tinted hair and a rather gushing manner. She was all sweetness to Ellie.

"You mustn't mind those letters I wrote you, Ellie," she said. "You must admit that it came as a terrible shock, your marrying like that. So secretly. But of course I know it was Greta who put you up to it, doing it that way."

"You mustn't blame Greta," said Ellie. "I didn't mean to upset you all so much. I just thought that—well, the less fuss—"

"Well, of course, Ellie dear, you have something there. All the men of business were simply livid—Stanford Lloyd and Andrew Lippincott. I suppose they thought everyone would blame them for not looking after you better. And of course they'd no idea of what Mike would be like. They didn't realize how charming he was going to be. I didn't myself." She smiled across at me, a very sweet smile and one of the falsest ones I'd ever seen! I thought to myself that if ever a woman hated a man, it was Cora who hated me. I thought her sweetness to Ellie was understandable enough. Andrew Lippincott had gone back to America and had, no doubt, given her a few words of caution. Ellie was selling some of her property in America, since she herself had definitely decided to live in England, but she was going to make a large allowance to Cora so that the latter could live where she chose. Nobody mentioned Cora's husband much. I gathered he'd already taken himself off to some other part of the world, and had not gone there alone. In all probability, I gathered, another divorce was pending. There wouldn't be much alimony out of this one. Cora's last marriage had been to a man a good many years younger than herself, with more attractions of a physical kind than cash.

Cora wanted that allowance. She was a woman of extravagant tastes. No doubt old Andrew Lippincott had hinted clearly enough that it could be discontinued any time if Ellie chose, or if Cora so far forgot herself as to criticize Ellie's new husband too virulently.

Cousin Reuben, or Uncle Reuben, did not make the journey. He wrote instead to Ellie a pleasant, noncommittal letter hoping she'd be very happy, but doubted if she would like living in England. "If you don't, Ellie, you come right back to the States. Don't think you won't get a welcome here, because you will. Certainly you will from your Uncle Reuben."

"He sounds rather nice," I said to Ellie.

"Yes," said Ellie meditatively. She wasn't, it seemed, quite so sure about it.

"Are you fond of any of them, Ellie?" I asked. "Or oughtn't I to ask you that?"

"Of course you can ask me anything." But she didn't answer for a moment or two, all the same. Then she said, with a sort of finality and decision, "No, I don't think I am. It seems odd, but I suppose it's because they don't really belong to me. Only by environment, not by relationship. They none of them are my flesh-and-blood relations. I loved my father, what I remembered of him. I think he was rather a weak man, and I think my grandfather was disappointed in him because he hadn't got much head for business. He didn't want to go into the business life. He liked going to Florida and fishing, that sort of thing. And then later he married Cora and I never cared for Cora much—or Cora for me, for that matter. My own mother, of course, I don't remember. I liked Uncle Henry and Uncle Joe. They were fun—in some ways more fun than my father was. He, I think, was in some ways a quiet and rather sad man. But the uncles enjoyed themselves. Uncle Joe was, I think, a bit wild, the kind that is wild just because they've got lots of money. Anyway, he was the one who got smashed up in the car, and the other one was killed fighting in the war. My grandfather was a sick man by that time, and it was a terrible blow to him that all his three sons were dead. He didn't like Cora and he didn't care much for any of his more distant relatives. Uncle Reuben, for instance. He said you could never tell what Reuben was up to. That's why he made arrangements to put his money in trust. A lot of it went to museums and hospitals. He left Cora well provided for, and his daughter's husband Uncle Frank."

"But most of it to you?"

"Yes. And I think that worried him a little bit. He did his best to get it looked after for me."

"By Uncle Andrew and by Mr. Stanford Lloyd. A lawyer and a banker."

"Yes. I suppose he didn't think I could look after it very well by myself. The odd thing is that he let me come into it at the age of twenty-one. He didn't keep it in trust till I was twenty-five, as lots of people do. I expect that was because I was a girl."

"That's odd," I said. "It would seem to me that it ought to be the other way round?"

Ellie shook her head. "No," she said, "I think my grandfather thought that young males were always wild and hit things up and that blondes with evil designs got hold of them. I think he though it would be a good thing if they had plenty of time to sow their wild oats. That's your English saying, isn't it? But he said once to me, 'If a girl is going to have any sense at all, she'll have it at twenty-one. It won't make any difference making her wait four years longer. If she's going to be a fool, she'll be a fool then just as much.' He said, too," Ellie looked at me and smiled, "that he didn't think I was a fool. He said, 'You mayn't know very much about life, but you've got good sense, Ellie. Especially about people. I think you always will have.'"

"I don't suppose he would have liked me," I said thoughtfully.

Ellie has a lot of honesty. She didn't try and reassure me by saying anything but what was undoubtedly the truth.

"No," she said, "I think he'd have been rather horrified. To begin with, that is. He'd have had to get used to you."

"Poor Ellie," I said suddenly.

"Why do you say that?"

"I said it to you once before, do you remember?"

"Yes. You said poor little rich girl. You were quite right, too."

"I didn't mean it the same way this time," I said. "I didn't mean that you were poor because you were rich. I think I meant—" I hesitated. "You've too many people," I said, "at you. All round you. Too many people who want things from you but who don't really care for you. That's true, isn't it?"

"I think Uncle Andrew really cares for me," said Ellie a little doubtfully. "He's always been nice to me, sympathetic. The others—no, you're quite right. They only want things."

"They come and cadge off you, don't they? Borrow

money off you, want favors. Want you to get them out of jams, that sort of thing. They're *at* you, *at* you, *at* you!"

"I suppose it's quite natural," said Ellie calmly, "but I've done with them all now. I'm coming to live here in England. I shan't see much of them."

She was wrong there, of course, but she hadn't grasped that fact yet. Stanford Lloyd came over later by himself. He brought a great many documents and papers and things for Ellie to sign and wanted her agreement on investments. He talked to her about investments and shares and property that she owned, and the disposal of trust funds. It was all double Dutch to me. I couldn't have helped her or advised her. I couldn't have stopped Stanford Lloyd from cheating her, either. I hoped he wasn't, but how could anyone ignorant like myself be sure?

There was something about Stanford Lloyd that was almost too good to be true. He was a banker, and he looked like a banker. He was rather a handsome man, though not young. He was very polite to me and thought dirt of me though he tried not to show it.

"Well," I said when he had finally taken his departure, "that's the last of the bunch."

"You didn't think much of any of them, did you?"

"I think your stepmother Cora is a double-faced bitch if I ever knew one. Sorry, Ellie, perhaps I oughtn't to say that."

"Why not, if that's what you think? I expect you're not far wrong."

"You must have been lonely, Ellie," I said.

"Yes, I was lonely. I knew girls of my own age. I went to a fashionable school but I was never really free. If I made friends with people, somehow or other they'd get me separated, push another girl at me instead. You know? Everything was governed by the social register. If I'd cared enough about anybody to make a fuss—but I never got far enough. There was never anybody I really cared for. Not until Greta came, and then everything was different. For the first time someone was really fond of me. It was wonderful." Her face softened.

"I wish," I said, as I turned away toward the window.

"What do you wish?"

"Oh, I don't know . . . I wish perhaps that you weren't —weren't quite so dependent on Greta. It's a bad thing to be as dependent as that on anyone."

"You don't like her, Mike," said Ellie.

"I do," I protested hurriedly. "Indeed I do. But you must realize, Ellie, that she is—well, she's quite a stranger to me. I suppose—let's face it—I'm a bit jealous of her. Jealous because she and you—well, I didn't understand before—how linked together you were."

"Don't be jealous. She's the only person who was good to me, who cared about me—till I met you."

"But you have met me," I said, "and you've married me." Then I said it again, what I'd said before, "And we're going to live together happily ever afterward."

13

I'm trying as best I can, though that isn't saying much, to paint a picture of the people who came into our lives, that is to say, who came into my life because, of course, they were in Ellie's life already. Our mistake was that we thought they'd go out of Ellie's life. But they didn't. They'd no intention of doing so. However, we didn't know that then.

The English side of our life was the next thing that happened. Our house was finished, we had a telegram from Santonix. He'd asked us to keep away for about a week, then the telegram came. It said, "Come tomorrow."

We drove down there, and we arrived at sunset. Santonix heard the car and came out to meet us, standing in front of the house. When I saw our house finished, something inside me leaped up, leaped up as though to burst out of my skin! It was my house—and I'd got it at last! I held Ellie's arm very tight.

"Like it?" said Santonix.

"It's the tops," I said. A silly thing to say, but he knew what I meant.

"Yes," he said, "it's the best thing I've done. . . . It's cost you a mint of money and it's worth every penny of it! I've exceeded my estimates all round. Come on, Mike," he said, "pick her up and carry her over the threshold. That's the thing to do when you enter into possession with your bride!"

I flushed and then I picked up Ellie—she was quite a lightweight—and carried her, as Santonix had suggested, over the threshold. As I did so, I stumbled just a little and I saw Santonix frown.

"There you are," said Santonix, "be good to her, Mike. Take care of her. Don't let any harm happen to her. She can't take care of herself. She thinks she can."

"Why should any harm happen to me?" said Ellie.

"Because it's a bad world and there are bad people in it," said Santonix, "and there are some bad people round you, my girl. I know. I've seen one or two of them. Seen them down here. They came nosing around, sniffing around like the rats they are. Excuse my French, but somebody's got to say it."

"They won't bother us," said Ellie; "they've all gone back to the States."

"Maybe," said Santonix, "but it's only a few hours by plane, you know."

He put his hands on her shoulders. They were very thin now, very white-looking. He looked terribly ill.

"I'd look after you myself, child, if I could," he said, "but I can't. It won't be long now. You'll have to fend for yourself."

"Cut out the gipsy's warning, Santonix," I said, "and take us round the house. Every inch of it."

So we went round the house. Some of the rooms were still empty, but most of the things we'd bought, pictures and the furniture and the curtains, were there.

"We haven't got a name for it," said Ellie suddenly. "We can't call it The Towers; that was a ridiculous name.

What was the other name for it that you told me once?" she said to me. "Gipsy's Acre, wasn't it?"

"We won't call it that," I said sharply. "I don't like that name."

"It'll always be called that hereabouts," said Santonix.

"They're a lot of silly superstitious people," I said.

And then we sat down on the terrace looking at the setting sun and the view, and we thought of names for the house. It was a kind of game. We started quite seriously and then we began to think of every silly name we possibly could. "Journey's End," "Heart's Delight," and names like boarding houses—"Seaview," "Fairholme," "The Pines." Then suddenly it grew dark and cold, and we went indoors. We didn't draw the curtains, just closed the windows. We'd brought down provisions with us. On the following day an expensively acquired domestic staff was coming.

"They'll probably hate it and say it's lonely and they'll all go away," said Ellie.

"And then you'll give them double the money to stay on," said Santonix.

"You think," said Ellie, "that everyone can be bought!" But she only said it laughingly.

We had brought *pâté en croûte* with us and French bread and large red prawns. We sat round the table laughing and eating and talking. Even Santonix looked strong and animated, and there was a kind of wild excitement in his eyes.

And then it happened suddenly. A stone crashed in through the window and dropped on the table. Smashed a glass too, and a sliver of glass slit Ellie's cheek. For a moment we sat paralyzed, then I sprang up, rushed to the window, unbolted it and went out on the terrace. There was no one to be seen. I came back into the room again.

I picked up a paper napkin and bent over Ellie, wiping away a little trickle of blood I saw coursing down her cheek.

"It's hurt you. . . . There, dear, it's nothing much. It's just a wee cut from a sliver of glass."

My eyes met those of Santonix.

"Why did anyone do it?" said Ellie. She looked bewildered.

"Boys," I said, "you know, young hooligans. They
knew, perhaps, we were settling in. I daresay you were
lucky that they only threw a stone. They might have had
an air gun or something like that."

"But why should they do it to us? Why?"

"I don't know," I said. "Just beastliness."

Ellie got up suddenly. She said,

"I'm frightened. I'm afraid."

"We'll find out tomorrow," I said. "We don't know
enough about the people round here."

"Is it because we're rich and they're poor?" said Ellie.
She asked it not of me but of Santonix, as though
he would know the answer to the quesion better than I
did.

"No," said Santonix slowly, "I don't think it's
that. . . ."

Ellie said,

"It's because they hate us. . . . Hate Mike and hate me.
Why? Because we're happy?"

Again Santonix shook his head.

"No," Ellie said, as though she were agreeing with him,
"no, it's something else. Something we don't know about.
Gipsy's Acre. Anyone who lives here is going to be hated.
Going to be persecuted. Perhaps they will succeed in the
end in driving us away. . . ."

I poured out a glass of wine and gave it to her.

"Don't, Ellie," I begged her. "Don't say such things.
Drink this. It's a nasty thing to happen, but it was only
silliness, crude horseplay."

"I wonder," said Ellie, "I wonder . . ." She looked
hard at me. "Somebody is trying to drive us away, Mike.
To drive us away from the house we've built, the house we
love."

"We won't let them drive us away," I said. I added,
"I'll take care of you. Nothing shall hurt you."

She looked again at Santonix.

"You should know," she said; "you've been here while
the house was building. Didn't anyone ever say anything

to you? Come and throw stones—interfere with the building of the house?"

"One can imagine things," said Santonix.

"There were accidents, then?"

"There are always a few accidents in the building of a house. Nothing serious or tragic. A man falls off a ladder, someone drops a load on his foot, someone gets a splinter in his thumb and it goes septic."

"Nothing more than that? Nothing that might have been meant?"

"No," said Santonix, *"no.* I swear to you, no!"

Ellie turned to me.

"You remember that gipsy woman, Mike. How queer she was that day, how she warned me not to come here."

"She's just a bit crazy, a bit off her head."

"We've built on Gipsy's Acre," said Ellie. "We've done what she told us not to do." Then she stamped her foot. "I won't let them drive me away. I won't let anyone drive me away!"

"Nobody shall drive us away," I said. "We're going to be happy here."

We said it like a challenge to fate.

14

■

That's how our life began at Gipsy's Acre. We didn't find another name for the house. That first evening fixed Gipsy's Acre in our heads.

"We'll call it Gipsy's Acre," said Ellie, "just to show! A kind of challenge, don't you think? It's our Acre, and to hell with the gipsy's warning."

She was her old gay self again the next day and soon we were busy getting ourselves settled in, and getting also to know the neighborhood and the neighbors. Ellie and I walked down to the cottage where the gipsy woman lived.

I felt it would be a good thing if we found her digging in her garden. The only time Ellie had seen her before was when she told our fortunes. If Ellie saw she was just an ordinary old woman—digging up potatoes—but we didn't see her. The cottage was shut up. I asked if she were dead, but the neighbor I asked shook her head.

"She must have gone away," she said. "She goes away from time to time, you know. She's a gipsy, really. That's why she can't stay in houses. She wanders away and comes back again." She tapped her forehead. "Not quite right up there."

Presently she said, trying to mask curiosity, "You've come from the new house up there, haven't you? The one on the top of the hill that's just been built."

"That's right," I said. "We moved in last night."

"Wonderful-looking place it is," she said. "We've all been up to look at it while it was building. Makes a difference, doesn't it, seeing a house like that where all those gloomy trees used to be." She said to Ellie rather shyly, "You're an American lady, aren't you, so we heard?"

"Yes," said Ellie, "I'm American—or I was, but now I'm married to an Englishman, so I'm an Englishwoman."

"And you've come here to settle down and live, haven't you?"

We said we had.

"Well, I hope you'll like it, I'm sure." She sounded doubtful.

"Why shouldn't we?"

"Oh, well, it's lonely up there, you know. People don't always like living in a lonely place among a lot of trees."

"Gipsy's Acre," said Ellie.

"Ah, you know the local name, do you? But the house that was there before was called The Towers. I don't know why. It hadn't got any towers, at least not in my time."

"I think The Towers is a silly name," said Ellie. "I think we'll go on calling it Gipsy's Acre."

"We'll have to tell the post office if so," I said, "or we shan't get any letters."

"No, I suppose we shan't."

"Though when I come to think of it," I said, "would

91

that matter, Ellie? Wouldn't it be much nicer if we didn't get any letters?"

"It might cause a lot of complications," said Ellie. "We shouldn't even get our bills."

"That would be a splendid idea," I said.

"No, it wouldn't," said Ellie. "Bailiffs would come in and camp there. Anyway," she said, "I wouldn't like not to get any letters. I'd want to hear from Greta."

"Never mind Greta," I said. "Let's go on exploring."

So we explored Kingston Bishop. It was a nice village, nice people in the shops. There was nothing sinister about the place. Our domestic help didn't take to it much, but we soon arranged that hired cars should take them into the nearest seaside town or into Market Chadwell on their days out. They were not enthusiastic about the location of the house, but it was not superstition that worried them. I pointed out to Ellie nobody could say the house was haunted because it had been just built.

"No," Ellie agreed, "it's not the house. There's nothing wrong with the house. It's outside. It's that road where it curves round through the trees and that bit of rather gloomy wood where that woman stood and made me jump so that day."

"Well, next year," I said, "we might cut down those trees and plant a lot of rhododendrons or something like that."

We went on making plans.

Greta came down and stayed with us for a weekend. She was enthusiastic about the house, and congratulated us on all our furnishings and pictures and color schemes. She was very tactful. After the weekend she said she wouldn't disturb the honeymooners any longer, and anyway she'd got to get back to her job.

Ellie enjoyed showing her the house. I could see how fond Ellie was of her. I tried to behave very sensibly and pleasantly, but I was glad when Greta went back to London, because her staying there had been a strain on me.

When we'd been there a couple of weeks, we were accepted locally and made the acquaintance of God. He came one afternoon to call upon us. Ellie and I were arguing about where we'd have a flower border when our correct, to me slightly phony-looking, manservant came out from the house to announce that Major Phillpot was in the drawing room. It was then that I said in a whisper to Ellie: "God!" Ellie asked me what I meant.

"Well, the locals treat him like that," I said.

So we went in and there was Major Phillpot. He was just a pleasant, nondescript man of close on sixty. He was wearing country clothes, rather shabby; he had gray hair going a little thin on top and a short bristly mustache. He apologized for his wife not being able to come and call on us. She was something of an invalid, he said. He sat down and chatted with us. Nothing he said was remarkable or particularly interesting. He had the knack of making people feel at their ease. He touched quite lightly on a variety of subjects. He didn't ask any direct questions, but he soon got it into his head where our particular interests lay. He talked to me about racing and to Ellie about making a garden and what things did well in this particular soil. He had been to the States once or twice. He found out that though Ellie didn't care much for race meetings, she was fond of riding. He told her that if she was going to keep horses, she could go up a particular track through the pine woods and she would come out on a good stretch of moor where she could have a good gallop. Then we came to the subject of our house and of the stories about Gipsy's Acre.

"I see you know the local name," he said, "and all the local superstitions, too, I expect."

"Gipsies' warnings in profusion," I said. "Far too many of them. Mostly old Mrs. Lee."

"Oh, dear," said Phillpot. "Poor old Esther. She's been a nuisance, has she?"

"Is she a bit dotty?" I asked.

"Not so much as she likes to make out. I feel more or less responsible for her. I settled her in that cottage," he said. "Not that she's grateful for it. I'm fond of the old thing, though she can be a nuisance sometimes."

"Fortunetelling?"

"No, not particularly. Why, has she told your fortune?"

"I don't know if you can call it a fortune," said Ellie. "It was more a warning to us against coming here."

"That seems rather odd to me." Major Phillpot's rather bristly eyebrows rose. "She's usually got rather a honeyed tongue in fortunes. Handsome stranger, marriage bells, six children and a heap of good fortune and money in your hand, pretty lady." He imitated rather unexpectedly the gipsy whine of her voice. "The gipsies used to camp here a lot when I was a boy," he said. "I suppose I got fond of them then, though they were a thieving lot, of course. But I've always been attracted to them. As long as you don't expect them to be law-abiding, they're all right. Many a tin mug of gipsy stew I've had as a schoolboy. We felt the family owed Mrs. Lee something; she saved the life of a brother of mine when he was a child. Fished him out of a pond when he'd gone through the ice."

I made a clumsy gesture and knocked a glass ashtray off a table. It smashed into fragments.

I picked up the pieces and Major Phillpot helped me.

"I expect Mrs. Lee's quite harmless, really," said Ellie. "I was very foolish to have been so scared."

"Scared, were you?" His eyebrows rose again. "It was as bad as that, was it?"

"I don't wonder she was afraid," I said quickly. "It was almost more like a threat than a warning."

"A threat!" He sounded rather incredulous.

"Well, it sounded that way to me. And then the first night we moved in here something else happened."

I told him about the stone crashing through the window.

"I'm afraid there are a good many young hooligans about nowadays," he said, "though we haven't got many of them round here—not nearly as bad as some places. Still, it happens, I'm sorry to say." He looked at Ellie. "I'm very sorry you were frightened. It was a beastly thing to happen, your first night moving in."

"Oh, I've got over it now," said Ellie. "It wasn't only that, it was—it was something else that happened not long afterward."

I told him about that, too. We had come down one

morning and we had found a dead bird skewered through with a knife and a small piece of paper with it which said in an illiterate scrawl, "Get out of here if you know what's good for you."

Phillpot looked really angry then. He said, "You should have reported that to the police."

"We didn't want to," I said. "After all, that would only have put whoever it is even more against us."

"Well, that kind of thing has got to be stopped," said Phillpot. Suddenly he became the magistrate. "Otherwise, you know, people will go on with the thing. Think it's funny, I suppose. Only—only this sounds a bit more than fun. Nasty—malicious— It's not," he said, rather as though he was talking to himself, "it's not as though anyone round here could have a grudge against you—a grudge against either of you personally, I mean."

"No," I said, "it couldn't be that because we're both strangers here."

"I'll look into it," Phillpot said.

He got up to go, looking round him as he did.

"You know," he said, "I like this house of yours. I didn't think I should. I'm a bit of an old square, you know, what used to be called an old fogy. I like old houses and old buildings. I don't like all these matchbox factories that are going up all over the country. Big boxes. Like beehives. I like buildings with some ornament on them, some grace. But I like this house. It's plain and very modern, I suppose, but it's got shape and light. And when you look out from it you see things—well, in a different way from the way you've seen them before. It's interesting. Very interesting. Who designed it? An English architect or a foreigner?"

I told him about Santonix.

"Hm," he said, "I think I read about him somewhere. Would it have been in *House and Gardens?* Some photographs and things."

I said he was fairly well known.

"I'd like to meet him sometime, though I don't suppose I'd know what to say to him. I'm not artistic."

Then he asked us to settle a day to come and have lunch with him and his wife.

"You can see how you like my house," he said.

"It's an old house, I suppose?" I said.

"Built 1720. Nice period. The original house was Elizabethan. That was burnt down about 1700 and a new one built on the same spot."

"You've always lived here, then?" I said. I didn't mean him personally, of course, but he understood.

"Yes. We've been here since Elizabethan times. Sometimes prosperous, sometimes down and out, selling land when things have gone badly, buying it back when things went well. I'll be glad to show it to you both," he said and, looking at Ellie, he added with a smile, "Americans like old houses, I know. You're the one who probably won't think much of it," he said to me.

"I won't pretend I know much about old things," I said.

He stumped off then. In his car there was a spaniel waiting for him. It was a battered old car with the paint rubbed off, but I was getting my values by now. I knew that in this part of the world he was still God, all right, and he'd set the seal of his approval on us. I could see that. He liked Ellie. I was inclined to think that he'd liked me, too, although I'd noticed the appraising glances which he shot over me from time to time, as though he was making a quick snap judgment on something he hadn't come across before.

Ellie was putting splinters of glass carefully in the wastepaper basket when I came back into the drawing room.

"I'm sorry it's broken," she said regretfully. "I liked it."

"We can get another like it," I said. "It's modern."

"I know! What startled you, Mike?"

I considered for a moment.

"Something Phillpot said. It reminded me of something that happened when I was a kid. A pal of mine at school and I played truant and went out skating on a local pond. Ice wouldn't bear us, silly little asses that we were. He went through and was drowned before anyone could get him out."

"How horrible."

"Yes. I'd forgotten all about it until Phillpot mentioned that about his own brother."

"I like him, Mike. Don't you?"

"Yes, very much. I wonder what his wife is like."

We went to lunch with the Phillpots early the following week. It was a white Georgian house, rather beautiful in its lines, though not particularly exciting. Inside, it was shabby but comfortable. There were pictures of what I took to be ancestors on the walls of the long dining room. Most of them were pretty bad, I thought, though they might have looked better if they had been cleaned. There was one of a fair-haired girl in pink satin that I rather took to. Major Phillpot smiled and said:

"You've picked one of our best. It's a Gainsborough, and a good one, though the subject of it caused a bit of trouble in her time. Strongly suspected of having poisoned her husband. May have been prejudice, because she was a foreigner. Gervase Phillpot picked her up abroad somewhere."

A few other neighbors had been invited to meet us—Dr. Shaw, an elderly man with a kindly but tired manner. He had to rush away before we had finished our meal. There was the Vicar, who was young and earnest, and a middle-aged woman with a bullying voice who bred corgis. And there was a tall, handsome, dark girl called Claudia Hardcastle, who seemed to live for horses, though hampered by having an allergy which gave her violent hay fever.

She and Ellie got on together rather well. Ellie adored riding and she, too, was troubled by an allergy.

"In the States it's mostly ragweed gives it to me," she said, "but horses, too, sometimes. It doesn't trouble me much nowadays because they have such wonderful things that doctors can give you for different kinds of allergies. I'll give you some of my capsules. They're bright orange. And if you remember to take one before you start out, you don't as much as sneeze once."

Claudia Hardcastle said that would be wonderful.

"Camels do it to me worse than horses," she said. "I

97

was in Egypt last year—and the tears just streamed down my face all the way round the Pyramids."

Ellie said some people got it with cats.

"And pillows." They went on talking about allergies.

I sat next to Mrs. Phillpot, who was tall and willowy and talked exclusively about her health in the intervals of eating a hearty meal. She gave me a full account of all her various ailments and of how puzzled many eminent members of the medical profession had been by her case. Occasionally she made a social diversion and asked me what I did. I parried that one, and she made half-hearted efforts to find out whom I knew. I could have answered truthfully "Nobody," but I thought it would be well to refrain —especially as she wasn't a real snob and didn't really want to know. Mrs. Corgi, whose proper name I hadn't caught, was much more thorough in her queries, but I diverted her to the general iniquity and ignorance of vets! It was all quite pleasant and peaceful, if rather dull.

Later, as we were making a rather desultory tour of the garden, Claudia Hardcastle joined me.

She said rather abruptly, "I've heard about you—from my brother."

I looked surprised. I couldn't imagine it to be possible that I knew a brother of Claudia Hardcastle's.

"Are you sure?" I said.

She seemed amused.

"As a matter of fact, he built your house."

"Do you mean Santonix is your brother?"

"Half brother. I don't know him very well. We rarely meet."

"He's wonderful," I said.

"Some people think so, I know."

"Don't you?"

"I'm never sure. There are two sides to him. At one time he was going right down the hill . . . People wouldn't have anything to do with him. And then—he seemed to change. He began to succeed in his profession in the most extraordinary way. It was as though he was—" she paused for a word—"dedicated."

"I think he is—just that."

Then I asked her if she had seen our house.

"No—not since it was finished."

I told her she must come and see it.

"I shan't like it, I warn you. I don't like modern houses. Queen Anne is my favorite period."

She said she was going to put Ellie up for the golf club. And they were going to ride together. Ellie was going to buy a horse—perhaps more than one. She and Ellie seemed to have made friends.

When Phillpot was showing me his stables, he said a word or two about Claudia.

"Good rider to hounds," he said. "Pity she's mucked up her life."

"Has she?"

"Married a rich man years older than herself. An American. Name of Lloyd. It didn't take. Came apart almost at once. She went back to her own name. Don't think she'll ever marry again. She's anti-man. Pity."

When we were driving home, Ellie said, "Dull—but nice. Nice people. We're going to be very happy here, aren't we, Mike?"

I said, "Yes, we are," and took my hand from the steering wheel and laid it over hers.

When we got back, I dropped Ellie at the house and put away the car in the garage.

As I walked back to the house, I heard the faint twanging of Ellie's guitar. She had a rather beautiful old Spanish guitar that must have been worth a lot of money. She used to sing to it in a soft, low, crooning voice. Very pleasant to hear. I didn't know what most of the songs were. American spirituals partly, I think, and some old Irish and Scottish ballads—sweet and rather sad. They weren't pop music or anything of that kind. Perhaps they were folk songs.

I went round by the terrace and paused by the window before going in.

Ellie was singing one of my favorites. I don't know what it was called. She was crooning the words softly to

99

herself, bending her head down over the guitar and gently plucking the strings. It had a sweet-sad haunting little tune.

> Man was made for Joy and Woe
> And when this we rightly know
> Thro' the World we safely go . . .
>
> Every Night and every Morn
> Some to Misery are born.
> Every Morn and every Night
> Some are born to Sweet Delight,
> Some are born to Endless Night. . . .

She looked up and saw me.

"Why are you looking at me like that, Mike?"

"Like what?"

"You're looking at me as though you loved me."

"Of course I love you. How else should I be looking at you?"

"But what were you thinking just then?"

I answered slowly and truthfully, "I was thinking of you as I saw you first—standing by a dark fir tree." Yes, I'd been remembering that first moment of seeing Ellie, the surprise of it and the excitement . . .

Ellie smiled at me and sang softly,

> Every Morn and every Night
> Some are born to Sweet Delight,
> Some are born to Sweet Delight,
> Some are born to Endless Night.

One doesn't recognize in one's life the really important moments—not until it's too late.

That day when we'd been to lunch with the Phillpots and came back so happily to our home was such a moment. But I didn't know it then—not until afterward.

I said, "Sing the song about the fly." And she changed to a gay little dance tune and sang,

Little Fly,
Thy Summer's play
My thoughtless hand
Has brushed away.

Am not I
A fly like thee?
Or art not thou
A man like me?

For I dance
And drink, and sing
Till some blind hand
Shall brush my wing.

If thought is life
And strength and breath
And the want
Of thought is death;

Then am I
A happy fly
If I live
Or if I die.

Oh, Ellie—Ellie . . .

15

It's astonishing in this world how things don't turn out at all the way you expect them to!

We'd moved into our house and were living there and we'd got away from everyone just the way I'd meant and planned. Only, of course, we hadn't got away from everyone. Things crowded back upon us across the ocean and in other ways.

First of all there was Ellie's blasted stepmother. She sent letters and cables and asked Ellie to go and see estate agents. She'd been so fascinated, she said, by our house that she really must have a house of her own in England. She said she'd love to spend a couple of months every year in England. And hard on her last cable she arrived and had to be taken round the neighborhood with lots of orders to view. In the end she more or less settled on a house—a house about fifteen miles away from us. We didn't want her there; we hated the idea—but we couldn't tell her so. Or rather, what I really mean is even if we had told her so, it wouldn't have stopped her taking it if she'd wanted it. We couldn't order her not to come there. It was the last thing Ellie wanted. I knew that. However, while she was still awaiting a surveyor's report, some cables arrived.

Uncle Frank, it seemed, had got himself into a jam of some kind. Something crooked and fraudulent, I gathered, which would mean a big sum of money to get him out. More cables passed to and fro between Mr. Lippincott and Ellie. And then there turned out to be some trouble between Stanford Lloyd and Lippincott. There was a row about some of Ellie's investments. I had felt, in my ignorance and credulity, that people who were in America were a long way away. I'd never realized that Ellie's relations and business connections thought nothing of taking a plane over to England for twenty-four hours and then flying back again. First Stanford Lloyd flew over and back again. Then Andrew Lippincott flew over.

Ellie had to go up to London and meet them. I hadn't got the hang of these financial things. I think everybody was being fairly careful in what they said. But it was something to do with the settling up of the trusts on Ellie, and a kind of sinister suggestion that either Mr. Lippincott had delayed the matter or it was Stanford Lloyd who was holding up the accounting.

In a lull between these worries Ellie and I discovered our Folly. We hadn't really explored all our property yet

102

(only the part just round the house). We used to follow up tracks through the woods and see where they led. One day we followed a sort of path that had been so overgrown that you couldn't really see where it was at first. But we tracked it out and in the end it came out at what Ellie said was a Folly—a sort of little white ridiculous temple-looking place. It was in fairly good condition, so we cleared it up and had it painted and we put a table and a few chairs in it and a divan and a corner cupboard in which we put china and glasses and some bottles. It was fun, really. Ellie said we'd have the path cleared and made easier to climb and I said no, it would be more fun if no one knew where it was except us. Ellie thought that was a romantic idea.

"We certainly won't let Cora know," I said, and Ellie agreed.

It was when we were coming down from there, not the first time but later, after Cora had gone away and we were hoping to be peaceful again, that Ellie, who was skipping along ahead of me, suddenly tripped over the root of a tree and fell and sprained her ankle.

Dr. Shaw came and said she'd taken a nasty sprain but that she'd be able to get about again all right in perhaps a week. Ellie sent for Greta then. I couldn't object. There was no one really to look after her properly—no woman, I mean. The servants we had were pretty useless, and anyway, Ellie wanted Greta. So Greta came.

She came and she was a great blessing, of course, to Ellie. And to me as far as that went. She arranged things and kept the household working properly. Our servants gave notice about now. They said it was too lonely—but really I think Cora had upset them. Greta put in advertisements and got another couple almost at once. She looked after Ellie's ankle, amused her, fetched things for her that she knew she liked, the kind of books and fruit and things like that—things I knew nothing about. And they seemed frightfully happy together. Ellie was certainly delighted to see Greta. And somehow or other Greta just didn't go away again. . . . She stopped on. Ellie said to me,

"You don't mind, do you, if Greta stays on for a bit?"

I said, "Oh, no. No, of course not."

"It's such a comfort having her," said Ellie. "You see, there are so many sort of female things we can do together. One's awfully lonely without another woman about."

Every day I noticed Greta was taking a bit more upon herself, giving orders, queening it over things. I pretended I liked having Greta there, but one day when Ellie was lying with her foot up inside the drawing room and Greta and I were out on the terrace, we suddenly got into a row together. I can't remember the exact words that started it. Something that Greta said, it annoyed me and I answered sharply back. And then we went on, hammer and tongs. Our voices rose. She let me have it, saying all the vicious, unkind things she could think of, and I pretty well gave her as good as I was getting. Told her she was a bossy, interfering female, that she'd far too much influence over Ellie, that I wasn't going to stand having Ellie bossed about the whole time. We shouted at each other and then suddenly Ellie came hobbling out on the terrace looking from one to the other of us, and I said,

"Darling, I'm sorry. I'm terribly sorry."

I went back into the house and settled Ellie on the sofa again. She said,

"I didn't realize. I didn't realize a bit that you—that you really hated having Greta here."

I soothed her and calmed her and said she mustn't take any notice, that I just lost my temper, that I was rather quarrelsome sometimes. I said all that was the matter was that I thought Greta was just a bit bossy. Perhaps that was natural enough because she'd been used to being so. And in the end I said I really liked Greta very much, it was just that I'd lost my temper because I'd been upset and worried. So it ended that I practically begged Greta to stay on.

It was quite a scene we'd had. I think quite a good many other people in the house had heard it as well. Our new manservant and his wife certainly did. When I get angry, I do shout. I daresay I really overdid it a bit. I'm like that.

Greta seemed to make a point of worrying a great deal about Ellie's health, saying she oughtn't to do this or that.

"She isn't really very strong, you know," she said to me.

"There's nothing wrong with Ellie," I said; "she's always perfectly well."

"No, she isn't, Mike. She's delicate."

When Dr. Shaw next came to have a look at Ellie's ankle and to tell her, by the way, that it was quite all right again, just bind it up if she was going to walk over rough ground, I said to him, I suppose in rather the foolish way that men do,

"She isn't delicate or anything, is she, Dr. Shaw?"

"Who says she's delicate?" Dr. Shaw was the kind of practitioner that is fairly rare nowadays and was, indeed, known locally as "Leave-it-to-Nature-Shaw."

"Nothing wrong with her as far as I can see," he said. "Anyone can sprain their ankle."

"I didn't mean her ankle. I wondered if she had a weak heart or anything like that."

He looked at me through the top of his spectacles. "Don't start imagining things, young man. What put it into your head? You're not the type that worries usually about women's ailments?"

"It was only what Miss Andersen said."

"Ah. Miss Andersen. What does she know about it? Not medically qualified, is she?"

"Oh, no," I said.

"Your wife's a woman of great wealth," he said, "according to local gossip, anyway. Of course some people just imagine all Americans are rich."

"She is wealthy," I said.

"Well, you must remember this. Rich women get the worst of it in many ways. Some doctor or other is always giving them powders and pills, stimulants or pep pills, or tranquilizers, things that on the whole they'd be better without. Now the village women are much healthier because nobody worries about their health in the same way."

"She does take some capsules or something," I said.

"I'll give her a check-up if you like. Might as well find out what muck she's been given. I can tell you, before now I've said to people, 'Chuck the whole lot in the waste-paper basket.' "

He spoke to Greta before he left. He said,

"Mr. Rogers asked me to give Mrs. Rogers a general check-up. I can't find anything much wrong with her. I think more exercises in the open air might do her good. What does she take in the way of medicines?"

"She has some tablets that she takes when she's tired, and some that she takes for sleeping if she wants them."

She and Dr. Shaw went and had a look at Ellie's prescriptions. Ellie was smiling a little.

"I don't take all these things, Dr. Shaw," she said. "Only the allergy capsules."

Shaw took a look at the capsules, read the prescription and said there was no harm in that, and passed on to a prescription for sleeping pills.

"Any trouble with sleeping?"

"Not living in the country. I don't think I've taken a single sleeping pill since I've been here."

"Well, that's a good thing." He patted her on the shoulder. "There's nothing wrong with you, my dear. Inclined to worry a bit sometimes, I should say. That's all. These capsules are mild enough. Lot of people take them nowadays and they don't do them any harm. Go on with them, but leave the sleeping pills alone."

"I don't know why I worried," I said to Ellie apologetically. "I suppose it was Greta."

"Oh," said Ellie, and laughed, "Greta fusses about me. She never takes any remedies herself." She said, "We'll have a turn-out, Mike, and throw most of these things away."

Ellie was getting on very friendly terms with most of our neighbors now. Claudia Hardcastle came over quite often, and she and Ellie went riding together occasionally. I didn't ride. I'd dealt with cars and mechanical things all my life. I didn't know the first thing about a horse in spite of mucking out stables in Ireland for a week or two once, but I thought to myself that sometime or other when we were in London I'd go to a posh riding stable and learn how to ride properly. I didn't want to start down here.

People would laugh at me, very likely. I thought riding was perhaps good for Ellie. She seemed to enjoy it.

Greta encouraged her to ride, although Greta herself also knew nothing about horses.

Ellie and Claudia went together to a sale, and on Claudia's advice Ellie bought herself a horse, a chestnut called Conquer. I urged Ellie to be careful when she went out riding by herself, but she laughed at me.

"I've ridden since I was three years old," she said.

So she usually went for a ride about two or three times a week. Greta used to drive the car and go into Market Chadwell to do the shopping.

One day Greta said at lunchtime, "You and your gipsies! There was a terrible-looking old woman this morning. She stood in the middle of the road. I might have run over her. Just stood smack in front of the car. I had to pull up. Coming up the hill, too."

"Why, what did she want?"

Ellie was listening to us both, but she didn't say anything. I thought, though, that she looked rather worried.

"Damn cheek; she threatened me," said Greta.

"Threatened you?" I said sharply.

"Well, she told me to get out of here. She said, 'This is gipsy land here. Go back. Go back, the lot of you. Go back to where you came from if you wish to be safe.' And she lifted up her fist and shook it at me. She said, 'If I curse you,' she said, 'there'll be no good luck for you ever again. Buying our land and raising houses on our land. We don't want houses where tent dwellers should be.' "

Greta said a lot more. Ellie said to me afterward, frowning a little,

"It all sounded most improbable, didn't you think so, Mike?"

"I think Greta was exaggerating a bit," I said.

"It didn't sound right somehow," said Ellie. "I wonder if Greta was making some of it up?"

I considered. "Why would she want to make things up?" Then I asked sharply, "You haven't seen our Esther lately, have you? Not when you are out riding?"

"The gipsy woman? No."

"You don't sound quite sure, Ellie," I said.

"I think I've caught glimpses of her," said Ellie. "You know, standing among the trees, peering out but never near enough for me to be sure."

But Ellie came back from a ride one day, white and shaking. The old woman had come out from in between the trees. Ellie had reined up and stopped to speak to her. She said the old woman was shaking her fist and muttering under her breath. Ellie said, "This time I was angry. I said to her,

" 'What do you want here? This land doesn't belong to you. It's our land and our house.' "

The old woman had said then,

"It'll never be your land and it'll never belong to you. I warned you once and I've warned you twice. I shan't warn you again. It won't be long now—I can tell you that. It's death I see. There behind your left shoulder. It's death standing by you, and it's death will have you. That horse you're riding has got one white foot. Don't you know that it's bad luck to ride a horse with one white foot? It's death I see and the grand house you've built falling in ruins!"

"This has got to be stopped," I said angrily.

Ellie didn't laugh it off this time. Both she and Greta looked upset. I went straight down to the village. I went first to Mrs. Lee's cottage. I hesitated for a moment but there was no light there and I went on to the police station. I knew the sergeant in charge—Sergeant Keene, a square, sensible man. He listened to me, then he said,

"I'm sorry you've had this trouble. She's a very old woman and she may be getting tiresome. We've never had much real trouble with her up to now. I'll speak to her and tell her to lay off."

"If you would," I said.

He hesitated a minute and then said,

"I don't like to suggest things—but as far as you know, Mr. Rogers, is there anyone around here who might—perhaps for some trivial cause—have it in for you or your wife?"

"I should think it most unlikely. Why?"

"Old Mrs. Lee has been flush of money lately—I don't know where it's coming from—"

"What are you suggesting?"

"It could be someone is paying her—someone who wants you out of here. There was an incident—a good many years ago. She took money from someone in the village—to frighten a neighbor away. Doing this same sort of stuff—threats—warnings—evil-eye business— Village people are superstitious. You'd be surprised at the number of villages in England that have got their private witch, so to speak. She got a warning then, and so far as I know she's never tried it on since—but it could be like that. She's fond of money— They'll do a lot for money—"

But I couldn't accept that idea. I pointed out to Keene that we were complete strangers here. "We've not had time to make enemies," I said.

I walked back to the house worried and perplexed. As I turned the corner of the terrace, I heard the faint sound of Ellie's guitar, and a tall figure, who had been standing by the window looking in, wheeled round and came toward me. For a moment I thought it was our gipsy, then I relaxed as I recognized Santonix.

"Oh," I said with a slight gasp, "it's you. Where have you sprung from? We've not heard from you for ages."

He didn't answer me directly. He just caught my arm and drew me away from the window.

"So she's here!" he said. "I'm not surprised. I thought she'd come sooner or later. Why did you let her? She's dangerous. You ought to know that."

"You mean Ellie?"

"No, no, not Ellie. The other one! What's her name? Greta."

I stared at him.

"Do you know what Greta's like, or don't you? She's come, hasn't she? Taken possession! You won't get rid of her now. She's come to stay."

"Ellie sprained her ankle," I said. "Greta came to look after her. She's—I suppose she's going soon."

"You don't know anything of the kind. She always

meant to come. I knew that. I took her measure when she came down while the house was building."

"Ellie seems to want her," I muttered.

"Oh, yes, she's been with Ellie some time, hasn't she? She knows how to manage Ellie."

That was what Lippincott had said. I'd seen for myself lately how true it was.

"Do you want her here, Mike?"

"I can't throw her out of the house," I said irritably. "She's Ellie's old friend. Her best friend. What the hell can I do about it?"

"No," said Santonix, "I suppose you can't do anything, can you?"

He looked at me. It was a very strange glance. Santonix was a strange man. You never knew what his words really meant.

"Do you know where you're going, Mike?" he said. "Have you any idea? Sometimes I don't think you know anything at all."

"Of course I know," I said. "I'm doing what I want to. I'm going where I wanted."

"Are you? I wonder. I wonder if you really know what you want yourself. I'm afraid for you with Greta. She's stronger than you are, you know."

"I don't see how you make that out. It isn't a question of strength."

"Isn't it? I think it is. She's the strong kind, the kind that always gets her way. You didn't mean to have her here. That's what you said. But here she is, and I've been watching them. She and Ellie sitting together, at home together, chattering and settled in. What are you, Mike? The outsider? Or aren't you an outsider?"

"You're crazy, the things you say. What do you mean— I'm an outsider? I'm Ellie's husband, aren't I?"

"Are you Ellie's husband or is Ellie your wife?"

"You're daft," I said. "What's the difference?"

He sighed. Suddenly, his shoulders sagged as though vigor went out of him.

"I can't reach you," said Santonix. "I can't make you

hear me. I can't make you understand. Sometimes I think you do understand, sometimes I think you don't know anything at all about yourself or anyone else."

"Look here," I said. "I'll take so much from you, Santonix. You're a wonderful architect—but—"

His face changed in the queer way it had.

"Yes," he said, "I'm a good architect. This house is the best thing I have done. I'm as near as possible satisfied with it. You wanted a house like this. And Ellie wanted a house like this, too, to live in with you. She's got it and you've got it. Send that other woman away, Mike, before it's too late."

"How can I upset Ellie?"

"That woman's got you where she wants you," said Santonix.

"Look here," I said, "I don't like Greta. She gets on my nerves. The other day I even had a frightful row with her. But none of it's as simple as you think."

"No, it won't be simple with her."

"Whoever called this place Gipsy's Acre and said it had a curse on it may have had something," I said angrily. "We've got gipsies who jump out from behind trees and shake fists at us and warn us that if we don't get out of here, some awful fate will happen to us. This place that ought to be good and beautiful."

They were queer words to say, those last ones. I said them as though it was somebody else saying them.

"Yes, it should be like that," said Santonix. "It should be. But it can't be, can it, if there is something evil possessing it?"

"You don't believe, surely, in—"

"There are many queer things I believe. . . . I know something about evil. Don't you realize, haven't you often felt, that I am partly evil myself? Always have been. That's why I know. I know when it's near me, although I don't always know exactly where it is. . . . I want the house I built purged of evil. You understand that?" His tone was menacing. "You understand that? It matters to me."

Then his whole manner changed.

"Come on," he said. "Don't let's talk a lot of nonsense. Let's come in and see Ellie."

So we went in through the window and Ellie greeted Santonix with enormous pleasure.

Santonix showed all his normal manner that evening. There were no more histrionics; he was his own self—charming, light-hearted. He talked mostly to Greta, giving her as it were the special benefit of his charm. And he had a lot of charm. Anyone would have sworn that he was impressed by her, that he liked her, that he was anxious to please her. It made me feel that Santonix was really a very dangerous man; there was a great deal more to him than I had ever glimpsed.

Greta always responded to admiration. She showed herself at her best. She could on occasions dim her beauty or else reveal it, and tonight she looked as beautiful as I'd ever seen her. Smiling at Santonix, listening to him as though spellbound. I wondered what lay behind his manner. You never knew with Santonix. Ellie said she hoped he was staying for several days, but he shook his head. He had to leave on the following day, he said.

"Are you building something now? Are you busy?"

He said no, he'd just come out of the hospital.

"They've patched me up once more," he said, "but it's probably for the last time."

"Patched you up? What do they do to you?"

"Drain the bad blood out of my body and put some good, fresh red blood in," he said.

"Oh." Ellie gave a little shudder.

"Don't worry," said Santonix, "it will never happen to you."

"But why has it got to happen to you?" said Ellie. "It's cruel."

"Not cruel, no," said Santonix. "I heard what you were singing just now.

> Man was made for Joy and Woe
> And when this we rightly know
> Thro' the World we safely go.

I go safely because I know why I'm here. And for you, Ellie,

> Every Morn and every Night
> Some are born to Sweet Delight.

That's you."

"I wish I could feel safe," said Ellie.

"Don't you feel safe?"

"I don't like to be threatened," said Ellie. "I don't like anyone to put a curse on me."

"You're talking about your gipsy?"

"Yes."

"Forget it," said Santonix. "Forget it for tonight. Let's be happy. Ellie—your health— Long life to you—and a quick and merciful end to me—and good luck to Mike here—" He stopped, his glass raised toward Greta.

"Yes?" said Greta. "And to me?"

"And to you, what's coming to you! Success, perhaps?" he added, half quizzically with an ironic question in his tone.

He went away next morning early.

"What a strange man he is," Ellie said. "I've never understood him."

"I never understand half of what he says," I answered.

"He knows things," said Ellie thoughtfully.

"You mean he knows the future?"

"No," said Ellie, "I didn't mean that. He knows people. I said it to you once before. He knows people better than they know themselves. Sometimes he hates them because of that, and sometimes he's sorry for them. He's not sorry for me, though," she added meditatively.

"Why should he be?" I demanded.

"Oh, because—" said Ellie.

■

16

It was the next day in the afternoon that as I was walking rather rapidly in the darkest part of the wood where the shade of the pine trees was more menacing than anywhere else, I saw the figure of a tall woman standing in the drive. I took a quick impulsive step off the path. I'd taken it for granted that she was our gipsy, but I stopped in sudden recoil when I saw who it actually was. It was my mother. She stood there tall and grim and gray-haired.

"Good Lord," I said, "you startled me, Mum. What are you doing here? Come to see us? We've asked you often enough, haven't we?"

We hadn't actually. I'd extended one rather lukewarm invitation, that was all. I'd put it, too, in a way which made it pretty sure that my mother wouldn't accept. I didn't want her here. I'd never wanted her here.

"You're right," she said. "I've come to see you at last. To see all's well with you. So this is the grand house you've built, and it is a grand house," she said, looking over my shoulder.

I thought I detected in her voice the disapproving acidity that I'd expected to find.

"Too grand for the likes of me, eh?" I said.

"I didn't say that, lad."

"But you thought it."

"It wasn't what you were born to, and no good comes from getting out of your station in life."

"Nobody'd ever get anywhere if they listened to you."

"Aye, I know that's what you say and think, but I don't know what good ambition's ever done to anybody. It's the kind of thing that turns to dead sea fruit in your mouth."

"Ah, for God's sake, don't croak," I said. "Come on. Come along up to see our grand house for yourself and turn up your nose at it. And come and see my grand wife, too, and turn up your nose at her if you dare."

"Your wife? I've seen her already."

"What do you mean, you've seen her already?" I demanded.

"So she didn't tell you, eh?"

"What?" I demanded.

"That she came to see me."

"She came to see you?" I asked, dumbfounded.

"Yes. There she was one day standing outside the door, ringing the bell and looking a little scared. She's a pretty lass and a sweet one for all the fine clothes she had on. She said, 'You're Mike's mother, aren't you?' and I said, 'Yes, and who are you?' and she said, 'I'm his wife.' She said, 'I had to come to see you. It didn't seem right that I shouldn't know Mike's mother. . . .' And I said, 'I bet he didn't want you to,' and she hesitated, and I said, 'You don't need to mind telling me that. I know my boy and I know what he'd want or not want.' She said, 'You think— perhaps he's ashamed of you because he and you are poor and I'm rich, but it isn't like that at all. That isn't like him at all. It isn't. Really, it isn't.' I said again, 'You don't need to tell me, lass. I know what faults my boy has. That's not one of his faults. He's not ashamed of his mother and he's not ashamed of his beginnings.

" 'He's not ashamed of me.' I said to her, 'He's afraid of me if anything. I know too much about him, you see.' And that seemed to amuse her. She said, 'I expect mothers always feel like that—that they know all about their sons. And I expect sons always feel embarrassed just because of that!'

"I said in a way that might be true enough. When you're young, you're always putting on an act to the world. I mind myself, when I was a child in my auntie's house. On the wall over my bed there was a great big eye in a gilt frame. It said, 'Thou God seest me.' Gave me the creeps, it did, all up my spine before I went to sleep."

"Ellie should have told me she'd been to see you," I said. "I don't see why she should keep it such a secret. She should have told me."

I was angry. I was very angry. I'd had no idea that Ellie would keep secrets like that from me.

"She was a little scared of what she'd done, maybe, but she'd no call to be frightened of you, my boy."

"Come on," I said, "come on and see our house."

I don't know whether she liked our house or not. I think not. She looked round the rooms and raised her eyebrows and then went into the terrace room. Ellie and Greta were sitting there. They'd just come in from outside and Greta had a scarlet wool cloak half over her shoulders. My mother looked at them both. She just stood there for a moment as though rooted to the spot. Ellie jumped up and came forward and across the room.

"Oh, it's Mrs. Rogers," she said. Then turning to Greta, "It's Mike's mother come to see our house and us. Isn't that nice? This is my friend Greta Andersen."

And she held out both her hands and took Mum's, and Mum looked at her and then looked over her shoulder at Greta very hard.

"I see," she said to herself, "I see."

"What do you see?" asked Ellie.

"I wondered," said Mum. "I wondered what it would all be like here." She looked round her. "Yes, it's a fine house. Fine curtains and fine chairs and fine pictures."

"You must have some tea," said Ellie.

"You look as if you've finished tea."

"Tea's a thing that need never be finished," said Ellie. Then she said to Greta, "I won't ring the bell. Greta, will you go out to the kitchen and make a fresh pot of tea?"

"Of course, darling," said Greta, and went out of the room looking over her shoulder once in a sharp, almost scared way at my mother.

My mother sat down.

"Where's your luggage?" said Ellie. "Have you come to stay? I hope you have."

"No, lass, I won't stay. I'm going back by train in half an hour's time. I just wanted to look in on you." Then she added rather quickly, probably because she wished to get it out before Greta came back, "Now don't worry yourself, love. I told him how you came to see me and paid me a visit."

"I'm sorry, Mike, that I didn't tell you," said Ellie firmly, "only I thought perhaps I'd better not."

"She came out of the kindness of her heart, she did," said my mother. "She's a good girl you've married, Mike, and a pretty one. Yes, a very pretty one." Then she added half audibly, "I am sorry."

"Sorry," said Ellie, faintly puzzled.

"Sorry for thinking the things I did," said my mother, and added with a slight air of strain, "Well, as you say, mothers are like that. Always inclined to be suspicious of daughters-in-law. But when I saw you, I knew he'd been lucky. It seemed too good to be true to me, that it did."

"What impertinence," I said, but I smiled at her as I said it. "I always had excellent taste."

"You've always had expensive taste, that's what you mean," said my mother, and looked at the brocade curtains.

"I'm not really the worse for being an expensive taste," said Ellie, smiling at her.

"You make him save a bit of money from time to time," said Mum; "it'll be good for his character."

"I refuse to have my character improved," I said. "The advantage of taking a wife is that the wife thinks everything you do is perfect. Isn't that so, Ellie?"

Ellie was looking happy again now. She laughed and said, "You're above yourself, Mike! The conceit of you."

Greta came back then with the teapot. We'd been a little ill at ease and we were just getting over it. Somehow when Greta came back the strain came on again. My mother resisted all endeavors on Ellie's part to make her stay over, and Ellie didn't insist after a short while. She and I walked down together with my mother along the winding drive through the trees and to the gateway.

"What do you call it?" my mother asked abruptly.

Ellie said, "Gipsy's Acre."

"Ah," said my mother, "yes, you've got gipsies around here, haven't you?"

"How did you know that?" I asked.

"I saw one as I came up. She looked at me queer, she did."

"She's all right, really," I said, "a little half baked, that's all."

"Why do you say she's half baked? She'd a funny look to her when she looked at me. She's got a grievance against you of some kind?"

"I don't think it's real," said Ellie. "I think she's imagined it all. That we've done her out of her land or something like that."

"I expect she wants money," said my mother. "Gipsies are like that. Make a big song and dance sometimes of how they've been done down one way or another. But they soon stop when they get some money in their itching palms."

"You don't like gipsies," said Ellie.

"They're a thieving lot. They don't work steady and they don't keep their hands off what doesn't belong to them."

"Oh, well," Ellie said, "we—we don't worry any more now."

My mother said good-by and then added, "Who's the young lady that lives with you?"

Ellie explained how Greta had been with her for three years before she married and how but for Greta she would have had a miserable life.

"Greta's done everything to help us. She's a wonderful person," said Ellie. "I wouldn't know how to—how to get on without her."

"She's living with you or on a visit?"

"Oh, well," said Ellie. She avoided the question. "She —she's living with us at present because I sprained my ankle and had to have someone to look after me. But I'm all right again now."

"Married people do best alone together when they're starting," my mother said.

We stood by the gate watching my mother march away down the hill.

"She's got a very strong personality," said Ellie thoughtfully.

I was angry with Ellie, really very angry because she'd gone and found out my mother and visited her without telling me. But when she turned and stood looking at me with one eyebrow raised a little and the funny half-timid, half-satisfied little-girl smile on her face, I couldn't help relenting.

"What a deceitful little thing you are," I said.

"Well," said Ellie, "I've had to be sometimes, you see."

"That's like a Shakespeare play I once saw. They did it at a school I was at." I quoted rather self-consciously, " 'She hath deceived her father and may deceive thee.' "

"What did you play—Othello?"

"No," I said, "I played the girl's father. That's why I remember that speech, I suppose. It's practically the only thing I had to say."

" 'She hath deceived her father and may deceive thee,' " said Ellie thoughtfully. "I didn't ever deceive my father as far as I know. Perhaps I would have later."

"I don't suppose he would have taken very kindly to your marrying me," I said, "any more than your stepmother did."

"No," said Ellie, "I don't suppose he would. He was pretty conventional, I think." Then she gave that funny little-girl smile again. "So I suppose I'd have had to be like Desdemona and deceived my father and run away with you."

"Why did you want to see my mother so much, Ellie?" I asked curiously.

"It's not so much I wanted to see her," said Ellie, "but I felt terribly bad not doing anything about it. You haven't mentioned your mother very often, but I did gather that she's always done everything she could for you. Come to the rescue about things and worked very hard to get you extra schooling and things like that. And I thought it seemed so mean and purse-proud of me not to go near her."

"Well, it wouldn't have been your fault," I said; "it would have been mine."

"Yes," said Ellie. "I can understand that perhaps you didn't want me to go and see her."

119

"You think I've got an inferiority complex about my mother? That's not true at all, Ellie. I assure you it isn't. It wasn't that."

"No," said Ellie thoughtfully, "I know that now. It was because you didn't want her to do a lot of mother stuff."

"Mother stuff?" I queried.

"Well," said Ellie, "I can see that she's the kind of person who would know quite well what other people ought to do. I mean, she'd want you to go in for certain kinds of jobs."

"Quite right," I said. "Steady jobs. Settling down."

"It wouldn't have mattered very much now," said Ellie. "I daresay it was very good advice. But it wouldn't have been the right advice ever for you, Mike. You're not a settler-down. You don't want to be steady. You want to go and see things and do things—be on top of the world."

"I want to stay here in this house with you," I said.

"For a while, perhaps . . . And I think—I think you'll always want to come back here. And so shall I. I think we shall come here every year, and I think we shall be happier here than anywhere else. But you'll want to go places, too. You'll want to travel and see things and buy things. Perhaps think up new plans for doing the garden here. Perhaps we'll go and look at Italian gardens, Japanese gardens, landscape gardens of all kinds."

"You make life seem very exciting, Ellie," I said. "I'm sorry I was cross."

"Oh, I don't mind your being cross," said Ellie. "I'm not afraid of you." Then she added, with a frown, "Your mother didn't like Greta."

"A lot of people don't like Greta," I said.

"Including you."

"Now look here, Ellie, you're always saying that. It's not true. I was just a bit jealous of her at first, that was all. We get on very well now." And I added, "I think perhaps she makes people get rather on the defensive."

"Mr. Lippincott doesn't like her either, does he? He thinks she's got too much influence over me," said Ellie.

"Has she?"

"I wonder why you should ask that. Yes, I think perhaps she has. It's only natural. She's rather a dominant personality and I had to have someone I could trust in and rely on. Someone who'd stand up for me."

"And see you got your own way?" I asked her, laughing.

We went into the house arm in arm. For some reason it seemed dark that afternoon. I suppose because the sun had just left the terrace and left a feeling of darkness behind it. Ellie said,

"What's the matter, Mike?"

"I don't know," I said. "Just suddenly I felt as though someone were walking over my grave."

"A goose is walking over your grave. That's the real saying, isn't it?" said Ellie.

Greta wasn't about anywhere. The servants said she'd gone out for a walk.

Now that my mother knew all about my marriage and had seen Ellie, I did what I had really wanted to do for some time. I sent her a large check. I told her to move into a better house and to buy herself any additional furniture she wanted. Things like that. I had doubts, of course, as to whether she would accept it or not. It wasn't money that I'd worked for and I couldn't honestly pretend it was. As I had expected, she sent the check back torn in two, with a scrawled note. "I'll have nought to do with any of this," she wrote. "You'll never be different. I know that now. Heaven help you." I flung it down in front of Ellie.

"You see what my mother's like," I said. "I married a rich girl, and I'm living on my rich wife's money and the old battleax disapproves of it!"

"Don't worry," said Ellie. "Lots of people think that way. She'll get over it. She loves you very much, Mike," she added.

"Then why does she want to alter me all the time? Make me into her pattern. I'm myself. I'm not anybody else's pattern. I'm not my mother's little boy to be molded the way she likes. I'm myself. I'm an adult. I'm me!"

"You're you," said Ellie, "and I love you."

And then, perhaps to distract me, she said something rather disquieting.

"What do you think," she said, "of this new manservant of ours?"

I hadn't thought about him. What was there to think? If anything, I preferred him to our last one, who had not troubled to conceal his low opinion of my social status.

"He's all right," I said. "Why?"

"I just wondered whether he might be a security man."

"A security man? What do you mean?"

"A detective. I thought Uncle Andrew might have arranged it."

"Why should he?"

"Well—possible kidnaping, I suppose. In the States, you know, we usually had guards—especially in the country."

Another of the disadvantages of having money that I hadn't known about!

"What a beastly idea!"

"Oh, I don't know. . . . I suppose I'm used to it. What does it matter? One doesn't really notice."

"Is the wife in it, too?"

"She'd have to be, I think, though she cooks very well. I should think that Uncle Andrew, or perhaps Stanford Lloyd, whichever one of them thought of it, must have paid our last ones to leave, and had these two all lined up ready to take their place. It would have been quite easy."

"Without telling you?" I was still incredulous.

"They'd never dream of telling me. I might have kicked up a fuss. Anyway, I may be quite wrong about them," she went on dreamily. "It's only that one gets a kind of feeling when one's been used to people of that kind always being around."

"Poor little rich girl," I said savagely.

Ellie did not mind at all.

"I suppose that does describe it rather well," she said.

"The things I'm learning about you all the time, Ellie," I said.

17

What a mysterious thing sleep is. You go to bed worrying about gipsies and secret enemies and detectives planted in your house and the possibilities of kidnaping and a hundred other things, and sleep whisks you away from it all. You travel very far and you don't know where you've been, but when you wake up, it's to a totally new world. No worries, no apprehensions. Instead, when I woke up on the 17th September, I was in a mood of boisterous excitement.

"A wonderful day," I said to myself with conviction. "This is going to be a wonderful day." I meant it. I was like those people in advertisements that offer to go anywhere and do anything. I went over plans in my head. I had arranged to meet Major Phillpot at a sale at a country house about fifteen miles away. They had some very nice stuff there and I'd already marked down two or three items in the catalogue. I was quite excited about the whole thing.

Phillpot was very knowledgeable about period furniture and silver and things of that kind, not because he was artistic—he was entirely a sporting man—but simply because he knew. His whole family was knowledgeable.

I looked over the catalogue at breakfast. Ellie had come down in a riding habit. She rode most mornings now—sometimes alone, sometimes with Claudia. She had the American habit of drinking coffee and a glass of orange juice and nothing much else for breakfast. My tastes now that I hadn't got to restrain them in any way were very much those of a Victorian squire! I liked lots of hot dishes on the sideboard. I ate kidneys this morning and sausages and bacon as well. Delicious.

"What are you doing, Greta?" I asked.

Greta said she was meeting Claudia Hardcastle at the

station at Market Chadwell and they were going up to London to a white sale. I asked what a white sale was.

"Does there really have to be white in it?" I asked.

Greta looked scornful and said that a white sale meant a sale of household linen and blankets and towels and sheets, etc. There were some very good bargains at a special shop in Bond Street, of which she had been sent a catalogue.

I said to Ellie, "Well, if Greta is going to London for the day, why don't you drive in and meet us at the George in Bartington? The food there's very good, so old Phillpot said. He suggested you might come. One o'clock. You go through Market Chadwell and then you take a turning about three miles after that. It's signposted, I think."

"All right," said Ellie, "I'll be there."

I mounted her and she went off riding through the trees. Ellie loved riding. She rode up one of the winding tracks and came out on the downs and had a gallop before returning home. I left the smaller car for Ellie, as it was easier to park, and took the big Chrysler myself. I got to Bartington Manor just before the sale began. Phillpot was there already and had kept a place for me.

"Some quite nice stuff here," he said. "One or two good pictures. A Romney and a Reynolds. I don't know if you're interested?"

I shook my head. My taste at the moment was entirely for modern artists.

"Several dealers here," Phillpot went on, "a couple down from London. See that thin man over there with the pinched lips? That's Cressington. Pretty well known. Not brought your wife?"

"No," I said, "she's not awfully keen on sales. Anyway, I didn't particularly want her to come this morning."

"Oh? Why not?"

"There's going to be a surprise for Ellie," I said. "Did you notice Lot Forty-two?"

He took a glance at the catalogue and then looked across the room.

"Hm. That papier-mâché desk? Yes. Rather a beautiful little piece. One of the best examples of papier-mâché

I've seen. Desk rather rare, too. Plenty of hand desks to stand on tables. But this is an early example. Never seen one quite like it before."

The little piece was inlaid with a design of Windsor Castle, and the sides of it had bouquets of roses and thistles and shamrock.

"Beautiful condition," said Phillpot. He looked at me curiously. "I shouldn't have thought it was your taste, but—"

"Oh, it isn't," I said. "It's a little too flowery and lady-like for me. But Ellie loves the stuff. It's her birthday next week and I want it as a present for her. A surprise. That's why I didn't want her to know I was bidding for it today. But I know there's nothing I could give her that she'd like more. She'll be really surprised."

We went in and took seats and the sale began. Actually, the piece I wanted was run up pretty high. Both the London dealers seemed keen on it, although one of them was so practiced and reserved about it that you could hardly notice the almost infinitesimal motion of his catalogue, which the auctioneer was observing closely. I bought a carved Chippendale chair as well, which I thought would look well in our hall, and some enormous brocade curtains in good condition.

"Well, you seem to have enjoyed yourself, all right," said Phillpot, rising to his feet when the auctioneer completed the morning's sale. "Want to come back this afternoon?"

I shook my head.

"No, there's nothing in the second half of the sale that I want. Mostly bedroom furniture and carpets and things like that."

"No, I didn't think you'd be interested. Well—" he looked at his watch—"we'd better be getting along. Is Ellie meeting us at the George?"

"Yes, she'll be there."

"And—er—Miss Andersen?"

"Oh, Greta's gone to London," I said. "She's gone to what they call a white sale. With Miss Hardcastle, I believe."

"Oh, yes, Claudia said something about it the other day. Prices of sheets and things are fantastic nowadays. Do you know what a linen pillow case costs? Thirty-five shillings. Used to buy 'em from six bob."

"You're very knowledgeable on household purchases," I said.

"Well, I hear my wife complaining about them." Phillpot smiled. "You're looking in the pink of condition, Mike. Happy as a sandboy."

"That's because I've got the papier-mâché desk," I said, "or, at any rate, that's partly it. I just woke up feeling happy this morning. You know those days when everything in the world seems right."

"Hm," said Phillpot, "be careful. That's what's known as being fey."

"Fey?" I said. "That's something Scottish, isn't it?"

"It comes before disaster, my boy," said Phillpot. "Better curb your exuberance."

"Oh, I don't believe those silly superstitions," I said.

"Nor in gipsies' prophecies, eh?"

"We haven't seen our gipsy lately," I said. "Well, not for a week at least."

"Perhaps she's away from the place," said Phillpot.

He asked me if I'd give him a lift in my car and I said I would.

"No use taking the two of them. You can drop me here on your way back, can't you? What about Ellie? Will she be bringing her car over?"

"Yes, she's bringing the little one."

"Hope the George will put on a good meal," said Major Phillpot. "I'm hungry."

"Did you buy anything?" I asked. "I was too excited to notice."

"Yes, you've got to keep your wits about you when you're bidding. Have to notice what the dealers are doing. No. I made a bid or two, but everything went far above my price."

I gathered that although Phillpot owned enormous quantities of land round about, his actual income did not amount to much. He was what you might describe as a poor man though a large landowner. Only by selling a good portion of his land would he have had money to spend, and he didn't want to sell his land. He loved it.

We got to the George and found a good many cars standing there already—possibly some of the people from the auction. I didn't see Ellie's, though. We went inside and I looked around for her, but she hadn't turned up yet. However, it was only just past one.

We went and had a drink at the bar while we were waiting for Ellie to arrive. The place was pretty crowded. I looked into the dining room, but they were still holding our table. There were a good many local faces that I knew, and sitting at a table by the window was a man whose face seemed familiar to me. I was sure I knew him but I couldn't remember when and where I'd met him. I didn't think he was a local. I was sure he was a stranger because his clothes didn't fit in with these parts. Of course I've knocked up against a great many people in my time and it is unlikely that I can remember them all easily. But this was a face, I thought, that I'd seen lately. I hadn't seen him at the sale as far as I could remember.

The presiding goddess of the George, rustling in her usual black silk of affected Edwardian style, which she always wore, came up to me and said,

"Will you be coming to your table soon, Mr. Rogers? There's one or two waiting."

"My wife will be here in a minute or two," I said.

I went back to rejoin Phillpot. I thought perhaps that Ellie might have had a puncture.

"We'd better go in," I said. "They seem getting rather upset about it. They've got quite a crowd today. I'm afraid," I added, "that Ellie isn't the most punctual of people."

"Ah," said Phillpot in his old-fashioned style, "the ladies make a point of keeping us waiting, don't they? All right, Mike, if that's all right by you. We'll go in and start lunch."

We went into the dining room, chose steak and kidney pie off the menu, and started.

"It's too bad of Ellie," I said, "to stand us up like this."

I added that it was possibly because Greta was in London. "Ellie's very used, you know," I said, "to Greta helping her to keep appointments, reminding her of them, and getting her off in time and all that."

"Is she very dependent on Miss Andersen?"

"In that way, yes," I said.

We went on eating and passed from the steak and kidney pie to apple tart with a self-conscious piece of phony pastry on top of it.

"I wonder if she's forgotten all about it, " I said suddenly.

"Perhaps you'd better ring up."

"Yes, I think I'd better."

I went out to the phone and rang. Mrs. Carson, the cook, answered.

"Oh, it's you, Mr. Rogers. Mrs. Rogers hasn't come home yet."

"What do you mean, hasn't come home? Home from where?"

"She hasn't come home from her ride yet."

"But that was after breakfast. She can't have been riding the whole morning."

"She didn't say anything different. I was expecting her back."

"Why didn't you ring up sooner and let me know about it?" I asked.

"Well, I wouldn't know where to get at you, you see. I didn't know where you'd gone."

I told her I was at the George at Bartington and gave her the number. She was to ring up the moment Ellie came in or she had news of her. Then I went back to join Phillpot. He saw from my face at once that something was wrong.

"Ellie hasn't come home," I said. "She went off riding this morning. She usually does most mornings, but it only lasts half an hour to an hour."

"Now don't worry before you need to, boy," he said kindly. "Your place is in a very lonely part, you know. Maybe her horse went lame and she might be walking it home. All that moorland and downs above the woods.

128

There's nobody much in that part to send a message by or anything like that."

"If she decided to change her plans and ride over and see anyone, anything like that," I said, "she'd have rung here. She'd have left a message for us."

"Well, don't get het up yet," Phillpot said. "I think we'd better go now, right away, and see what we can find out."

As we went out to the car park, another car drove away. In it was the man I had noticed in the dining room and suddenly it came to me who it was. Stanford Lloyd or someone just like him. I wondered what he could be doing down here. Could he be coming to see us? If so, it was odd he hadn't let us know. In the car with him was a woman who had looked like Claudia Hardcastle, but surely she was in London with Greta, shopping. It all floored me rather . . .

As we drove away, Phillpot looked at me once or twice. I caught his eye once and said rather bitterly,

"All right. You said I was fey this morning."

"Well, don't think of that yet. She may have had a fall and sprained an ankle or something like that. She's a good horsewoman, though," he said. "I've seen her. I can't feel an accident is really likely."

I said, "Accidents can happen at any time."

We drove fast and came at last to the road over the downs above our property, looking about us as we went. Now and again we stopped to ask people. We stopped a man who was digging peat and there we got the first news.

"Seen a riderless horse I have," he said. "Two hours ago maybe or longer. I would-a caught it but it galloped off when I got near it. Didn't see anyone though."

"Best drive home," suggested Phillpot; "there may be news of her there."

We drove home but there was no news. We got hold of the groom and sent him off to ride over the moorland in search of Ellie. Phillpot telephoned his own house and sent a man from there, too. He and I went up a path together and through the wood, the one that Ellie often took, and came out on the downs there.

At first there was nothing to be seen. Then we walked along the edge of the wood near where some of the other paths came out and so—we found her. We saw what looked like a huddled heap of clothes. The horse had come back and was now standing cropping near that huddled heap. I began to run. Phillpot followed me faster than I'd have thought a man of his age could have kept up.

She was there—lying in a crumpled-up heap, her little white face turned up to the sky. I said,

"I can't—I can't—" and turned my face away.

Phillpot went and knelt down by her. He got up almost at once.

"We'll get hold of a doctor," he said. "Shaw. He's the nearest. But—I don't think it's any use, Mike."

"You mean—she's dead?"

"Yes," he said, "it's no good pretending anything else."

"Oh, God!" I said, and turned away. "I can't believe it. Not Ellie."

"Here, have this," said Phillpot.

He took a flask out of his pocket, unscrewed it and handed it to me. I took a good deep pull at it.

"Thanks," I said.

The groom came along then, and Phillpot sent him off to fetch Dr. Shaw.

18

Shaw came up in a battered old Landrover—I suppose the car he used for going to visit isolated farms in bad weather. He barely looked at either of us. He went straight and bent over Ellie. Then he came over to us.

"She's been dead at least three or four hours," he said. "How did it happen?"

I told him how she'd gone off riding as usual after breakfast that morning.

"Has she had any accidents up to this time when she's been out riding?"

"No," I said, "she was a good rider."

"Yes, I know she's a good rider. I've seen her once or twice. She's ridden since she was a child, I understand. I wondered if she might have had some accident lately and that that might have affected her nerve a bit. If the horse had shied—"

"Why should the horse shy? It's a quiet brute—"

"There's nothing vicious about this particular horse," said Major Phillpot. "He's well behaved, not nervy. Has she broken any bones?"

"I haven't made a complete examination yet, but she doesn't seem physically injured in any way. There may be some internal injury. Might be shock, I suppose."

"But you can't die of shock," I said.

"People have died of shock before now. If she'd had a weak heart—"

"They said in America that she had a weak heart—some kind of weakness at least."

"Hm. I couldn't find much trace of it when I examined her. Still, we didn't have a cardiograph. Anyway, no point in going into that now. We shall know later. After the inquest."

He looked at me consideringly, then he patted me on the shoulder.

"You go home and go to bed," he said. "You're the one who's suffering from shock."

In the queer way people materialize out of nowhere in the country, we had three or four people standing by, by this time—one a hiker who had come along from the main road seeing our little group, one a rosy-faced woman who I think was going to a farm over a short cut, and an old road man. They were making exclamations and remarks.

"Poor young lady."

"So young, too. Thrown from her horse, was she?"

"Ah, well, you never know with horses."

"It's Mrs. Rogers, isn't it? The American lady from The Towers?"

It was not until everyone else had exclaimed in their astonished fashion that the aged road man spoke. He gave us information. Shaking his head, he said,

"I musta seen it happen. I musta seen it happen."

The doctor turned sharply on him.

"What did you see happen?"

"I saw a horse bolting across country."

"Did you see the lady fall?"

"No. No, I didn't. She were riding along the top of the woods when I saw her and after that I'd got me back turned and I was cutting stones for the road. And then I heard hoofs and I looked up and there was the horse agalloping. I didn't think there'd been an accident. I thought the lady perhaps had got off and let go of the horse in some way. It wasn't coming toward me; it was going in the other direction."

"You didn't see the lady lying on the ground?"

"No, I don't see very well far. I saw the horse because it showed against the sky-line."

"Was she riding alone? Was there anyone with her, or near her?"

"Nobody near her. No. She was all alone. She rode not very far from me, past me, going along that way. She was bearing toward the woods, I think. No, I didn't see anyone at all except her and the horse."

"Might have been the gipsy what frightened her," said the rosy-faced woman.

I swung round.

"What gipsy? When?"

"Oh, must have been—well, it must have been three or four hours ago when I went down the road this morning. About quarter to ten maybe, I saw that gipsy woman. The one as lives in the cottage in the village. Least I think it was she. I wasn't near enough to be sure. But she's the only one as goes about hereabouts in a red cloak. She was walking up a path through the trees. Somebody told me as she'd said nasty things to the poor American young lady. Threatened her. Told her something bad would happen if she didn't get out of this place. Very threatening, I hear she was."

"The gipsy," I said. Then, bitterly, to myself, though out loud, "Gipsy's Acre. I wish I'd never seen the place."

BOOK THREE

19

It's extraordinary how difficult it is for me to remember what happened after that—I mean, the sequence of it all. Up to then, you see, it's all clear in my mind. I was a little doubtful where to begin, that was all. But from then on it was as though a knife fell, cutting my life into two halves. What I went on to from the moment of Ellie's death seems to me now like something for which I was not prepared. A confusion of thrusting people and elements and happenings where I wasn't myself in control of anything any more. Things happened not to me, but all around me. That's what it seemed like.

Everybody was very kind to me. That seems the thing I remember best. I stumbled about and looked dazed and didn't know what to do. Greta, I remember, came into her element. She had that amazing power that women have to take charge of a situation and deal with it. Deal, I mean, with all the small unimportant details that someone has to see to. I would have been incapable of seeing to them.

I think the first thing I remembered clearly after they'd taken Ellie away and I'd got back to my house—our house—*the* house—was when Shaw came along and talked to me. I don't know how long after that was. He was quiet, kind, reasonable—just explaining things clearly and gently.

Arrangements. I remember his using the word arrangements. What a hateful word it is. All the things it stands for. All the things in life that have grand words. Love—sex—life—death—hate. Those aren't the things that govern existence at all. It's lots of other pettifogging, degrading things. Things you have to endure, things you never think about until they happen to you. Undertakers, arrangements for funerals. And servants coming into rooms and pulling the blinds down. Why should blinds be pulled down because Ellie was dead? Of all the stupid things!

That was why, I remember, I felt quite grateful to Dr. Shaw. He dealt with such things so kindly and sensibly, explaining gently why certain things had to be—talking rather slowly, I remember, so that he could be quite sure I was taking them in.

I didn't know what an inquest would be like. I'd never been to one. It seemed to me curiously unreal, amateurish. The coroner was a small fussy little man with pince-nez. I had to give evidence of identification, to describe the last time I had seen Ellie at the breakfast table, and her departure for her usual morning ride and the arrangement we had made to meet later for lunch. She had seemed, I said, exactly the same as usual, in perfectly good health.

Dr. Shaw's evidence was quiet, inconclusive. No serious injuries, a wrenched collar bone and bruises such as would result from a fall from the horse, not of a very serious nature, and inflicted at the time of death. She did not appear to have moved again after she had fallen. Death, he thought, had been practically instantaneous. There was no specific injury to have caused death, and he could give no other explanation of it than she had died from heart failure caused by shock. As far as I could make out from the medical language used, Ellie had died simply as the result of absence of breath—of asphyxia of some kind. Her organs were healthy, her stomach contents normal.

Greta, who also gave evidence, stressed rather more forcibly than she had done to Dr. Shaw before that Ellie had suffered from some form of heart malady three or four years ago. She had never heard anything definite mentioned, but Ellie's relations had occasionally said that her heart was weak and that she must take care not to overdo things. She had never heard anything more definite than that.

Then we came to the people who had seen or been in the vicinity at the time the accident happened. The old man who had been cutting peat was the first of them. He had seen the lady pass him; she'd been about fifty yards or so away. He knew who she was, though he'd never spoken to her. She was the lady from the new house.

"You knew her by sight?"

"No, not exactly by sight, but I knew the horse, sir. It's got a white fetlock. Used to belong to Mr. Carey over at Shettlegroom. I've never heard it's anything but quiet and well behaved, suitable for a lady to ride."

"Was the horse giving any trouble when you saw it? Playing up in any way?"

"No, it was quiet enough. It was a nice morning."

There had not been many people about, he said. He hadn't noticed many. That particular track across the moor wasn't much used except as a short cut occasionally to one of the farms. Another track crossed it about a mile further away. He'd seen one or two passers-by that morning, but not to notice—one man on a bicycle, another man walking. They were too far away for him to see who they were, and he hadn't noticed much, anyway. Earlier, he said, before he'd seen the lady riding, he'd seen old Mrs. Lee, or so he thought. She was coming up the track toward him, and then she turned off and went into the woods. She often walked across the moors and in and out of the woods.

The coroner asked why Mrs. Lee was not in court. He understood that she'd been summoned to attend. He was told, however, that Mrs. Lee had left the village some days ago—nobody knew exactly when. She had not left any address behind. It was not her habit to do so; she often went away and came back without notifying anyone, so there was nothing unusual about this. In fact one or two people said they thought she'd already left the village before the day the accident happened. The coroner asked the old man again.

"You think, however, that it was Mrs. Lee you saw?"

"Couldn't say, I'm sure. Wouldn't like to be certain. It was a tall woman and striding along, and had on a scarlet cloak like Mrs. Lee wears sometimes. But I didn't look particular. I was busy with what I was doing. Could have been she, it could have been someone else. Who's to say?"

As for the rest, he repeated very much what he had said to us. He'd seen the lady riding nearby, he'd often seen her riding before. He hadn't paid any particular attention. Only later did he see the horse galloping alone. It looked as though something had frightened it, he said. "At least, it could be that way." He couldn't tell what time that was. Might have been eleven, might have been earlier. He saw the horse much later, further away. It seemed to be returning toward the woods.

Then the coroner recalled me and asked me a few more questions about Mrs. Lee—Mrs. Esther Lee of Vine Cottage.

"You and your wife knew Mrs. Lee by sight?"

"Yes," I said, "quite well."

"Did you talk with her?"

"Yes, several times. Or rather," I added, "she talked to us."

"Did she at any time threaten you or your wife?"

I paused a moment or two.

"In a sense she did," I said slowly, "but I never thought—"

"You never thought what?"

"I never thought she really meant it," I said.

"Did she sound as though she had any particular grudge against your wife?"

"My wife said so once. She said she thought she had some special grudge against her, but she couldn't see why."

"Had you or your wife at any time ordered her off your land, threatened her, treated her roughly in any way?"

"Any aggression came from her side," I said.

"Did you ever have the impression that she was mentally unbalanced?"

I considered. "Yes," I said, "I did. I thought she had come to believe that the land on which we had built our house belonged to her, or belonged to her tribe or whatever they call themselves. She had a kind of obsession about it." I added slowly, "I think she was getting worse, more and more obsessed by the idea."

"I see. She never offered your wife physical violence at any time?"

"No," I said slowly, "I don't think it would be fair to say that. It was all—well, all a sort of gipsy's warning stuff. 'You'll have bad luck if you stay here.' 'There'll be a curse on you unless you go away.' "

"Did she mention the word death?"

"Yes, I think so. We didn't take her seriously. At least," I corrected myself, "I didn't."

"Do you think your wife did?"

"I'm afraid she did sometimes. The old woman, you know, could be rather alarming. I don't think she was really responsible for what she was saying or doing."

The preceedings ended with the coroner adjourning the inquest for a fortnight. Everything pointed to death being due to accidental causes, but there was not sufficient evidence to show what had caused the accident to occur. He would adjourn the proceedings until he had heard the evidence of Mrs. Esther Lee.

■

20

The day after the inquest I went to see Major Phillpot and I told him point-blank that I wanted his opinion. Someone whom the old peat-cutting man had taken to be Mrs. Esther Lee had been seen going up toward the woods that morning.

"You know the old woman," I said. "Do you actually think that she would have been capable of causing an accident by deliberate malice?"

"I can't really believe so, Mike," he said. "To do a thing like that you need a very strong motive—revenge for some personal injury caused to you. Something like that. And what has Ellie ever done to her? Nothing."

"It seems crazy, I know. Why was she constantly appearing in that queer way, threatening Ellie, telling her to go away? She seemed to have a grudge against her, but how could she have a grudge? She'd never met Ellie or seen her before. What was Ellie to her but a perfectly strange American? There's no past history, no link between them."

"I know, I know," said Phillpot. "I can't help feeling, Mike, that there's something here that we don't understand. I don't know how much your wife was over in England previous to her marriage. Did she ever live in this part of the world for any length of time?"

"No, I'm sure of that. It's all so difficult. I don't really know anything about Ellie. I mean, who she knew, where she went. We just—met." I checked myself and looked at him. I said, "You don't know how we came to meet, do you? No," I went on, "you wouldn't guess in a hundred years how we met." And suddenly, in spite of myself, I began to laugh. Then I pulled myself together. I could feel that I was very near hysteria.

I could see his kind patient face just waiting till I was

myself again. He was a helpful man. There was no doubt of that.

"We met here," I said. "Here at Gipsy's Acre. I had been reading the notice board of the sale of The Towers and I walked up the road, up the hill, because I was curious about this place. And that's how I first saw her. She was standing there under a tree. I startled her—or perhaps it was she who startled me. Anyway, that's how it all began. That's how we came to live here in this damned, cursed, unlucky place."

"Have you felt that all along, that it would be unlucky?"

"No. Yes. No, I don't know, really. I've never admitted it. I've never wanted to admit it. But I think she knew. I think she's been frightened all along." Then I said slowly, "I think somebody deliberately wanted to frighten her."

He said rather sharply, "What do you mean by that? Who wanted to frighten her?"

"Presumably the gipsy woman. But somehow I'm not quite sure about it. . . . She used to lie in wait for Ellie, you know, tell her this place would bring her bad luck. Tell her she ought to go away from it."

"Tcha!" He spoke angrily. "I wish I'd been told more about that. I'd have spoken to old Esther. Told her she couldn't do things like that."

"Why did she?" I asked. "What made her?"

"Like so many people," said Phillpot, "she likes to make herself important. She likes either to give people warnings or else tell their fortunes and prophesy happy lives for them. She likes to pretend she knows the future."

"Supposing," I said slowly, "somebody gave her money. I've been told she's fond of money."

"Yes, she was very fond of money. If someone paid her —that's what you're suggesting? What put that idea into your head?"

"Sergeant Keene," I said. "I should never have thought of it myself."

"I see." He shook his head doubtfully.

"I can't believe," he said, "that she would deliberately

140

try to frighten your wife to the extent of causing an accident."

"She mayn't have counted on a fatal accident. She might have done something to frighten the horse," I said, "let off a squib or flapped a sheet of white paper or something. Sometimes, you know, I did feel that she had some entirely personal grudge against Ellie, a grudge for some reason that I don't know about."

"That sounds very far-fetched."

"This place never belonged to her?" I asked. "The land, I mean."

"No. Gipsies may have been warned off this property probably more than once. Gipsies are always getting turned off places, but I doubt if they keep up a lifelong resentment about it."

"No," I said, "that would be far-fetched. But I do wonder if for some reason that we don't know about—she was?"

"A reason we don't know about—what reason?"

I reflected a moment or two.

"Everything I say will just sound fantastic. Let's say that, as Keene suggested, someone paid her to do the things she did. What did that someone want? Say they wanted to make us both go away from here. They concentrated on Ellie, not on me, because I wouldn't be scared in the way Ellie would be. They frightened her to get her—and through her both of us—to leave here. If so, there must be some reason for wanting the land to come on the market again. Somebody, shall we say, for some reason wants our land." I stopped.

"It's a logical suggestion," Phillpot said, "but I know of no reason why anyone should."

"Some important mineral deposit," I suggested, "that nobody knows about."

"Hm, I doubt it."

"Something like buried treasure. Oh, I know it sounds absurd. Or—well, say the proceeds of some big bank robbery."

Phillpot was still shaking his head but rather less vehemently now.

"The only other proposition," I said, "is to go one step farther back as you did just now—behind Mrs. Lee to the person who paid Mrs. Lee. That might be some unknown enemy of Ellie's."

"But you can't think of anyone it would be likely to be?"

"No. She didn't know anyone down here. That I'm sure of. She had no links with this place." I got up. "Thank you for listening to me," I said.

"I wish I could have been more helpful."

I went out of the door, fingering the thing that I was carrying in my pocket. Then, taking a sudden decision, I turned on my heel and went back into the room.

"There's something I'd like to show you," I said. "Actually, I was going to take it down to show to Sergeant Keene and see what he could make of it."

I dived into my pocket and brought out a stone round which was wrapped a crumpled bit of paper with printed writing on it.

"This was thrown through our breakfast window this morning," I said. "I heard the crash of the glass as I came down the stairs. A stone was thrown through the window once before when we first came here. I don't know if this is the same person or not."

I took off the wrapping paper and held it out to him. It was a dirty, coarse bit of paper. There was some printing on it in rather faint ink. Phillpot put on his spectacles and bent over the piece of paper. The message on it was quite short. All it said was, *It was a woman who killed your wife.*

Phillpot's eyes went up.

"Extraordinary," he said. "Was the first message you got printed?"

"I can't remember now. It was just a warning to go away from here. I can't even remember the exact wording of it now. Anyway, it seems pretty certain that that was hooligans. This doesn't seem quite the same."

"Do you think it was thrown in by someone who knew something?"

"Probably just a bit of silly cruel malice in the anonymous letter class. You get it, you know, a good deal in villages."

He handed it back to me.

"But I think your instinct was right," he said, "to take it to Sergeant Keene. He'll know more about these anonymous things than I should."

I found Sergeant Keene at the police station, and he was definitely interested.

"There's queer things going on here," he said.

"What do you think it means?" I asked.

"Hard to say. Might be just malice leading up to accusing some particular person."

"It might be just accusing Mrs. Lee, I suppose?"

"No, I don't think it would have been put that way. It might be—I'd like to think it was—it might be that someone saw or heard something—heard a noise or a cry or the horse bolted right past someone, and they saw or met a woman soon afterward. But it sounds as though it was a different woman from the gipsy, because everyone thinks the gipsy's mixed up in this anyway. So this sounds as though another, an entirely different woman was meant."

"What about the gipsy?" I said. "Have you had news of her, found her?"

He shook his head slowly.

"We know some of the places she used to go when she left here. East Anglia, that way. She'd friends there among the gipsy clan. She's not been there, they say, but they'd say that anyway. They clam up, you know. She's fairly well known by sight in those parts, but nobody's seen her. All the same, I don't think she's as far away as East Anglia."

There was something peculiar about the way he said the words.

"I don't quite understand," I said.

"Look at it this way. She's scared. She's got good reason to be. She's been threatening your wife, frightening her, and now, say, she caused an accident and your wife died. The police'll be after her. She knows that, so she'll go to earth, as you might say. She'll put as big a distance between herself and us as she possibly can. But she won't want to show herself. She'd be afraid of public transport."

"But you'll find her? She's a woman of striking appearance."

"Ah, yes, we shall find her eventually. These things take a little time. That is if it was that way."

"But you think it was some other way."

"Well, you know what I've wondered all along. Whether somebody was paying her to say the things she did."

"Then she might be even more anxious to get away," I said.

"But somebody else would be anxious, too. You've got to think of that, Mr. Rogers."

"You mean," I said slowly, "the person who paid her."

"Yes."

"Supposing it was a—a woman who paid her."

"And supposing somebody has some idea of that. And so they start sending anonymous messages. That woman would be scared, too. She needn't have meant this to happen, you know. However much she got that gipsy woman to frighten your wife away from this place, she wouldn't have meant it to result in Mrs. Roger's death."

"No," I said. "Death wasn't meant. It was just to frighten us—to frighten my wife and to frighten me into leaving here."

"And now who's going to be frightened? The woman who caused the accident. And that's Mrs. Esther Lee. And so she's going to come clean, isn't she? Say it wasn't really her doing. She'll admit even that she was paid money to do it. And she'll mention a name. She'll say who paid her. And somebody wouldn't like that, would they, Mr. Rogers?"

"You mean this unknown woman that we've more or less postulated without even knowing there's any such person?"

"Man or woman, say someone paid her. Well, that someone would want her silenced pretty quickly, wouldn't they?"

"You're thinking she might be dead?"

144

"It's a possibility, isn't it?" said Keene. Then he made what seemed quite an abrupt change of subject. "You know that kind of Folly place, Mr. Rogers, that you've got up at the top of your woods?"

"Yes," I said, "what of it? My wife and I had it repaired and fixed up a bit. We used to go up there occasionally but not very often. Not lately certainly. Why?"

"Well, we've been hunting about, you know. We looked into this Folly. It wasn't locked."

"No," I said, "we never bothered to lock it. There was nothing of value in there, just a few odd bits of furniture."

"We thought it possible old Mrs. Lee had been using it, but we found no traces of her. We did find this, though. I was going to show it to you anyway." He opened a drawer and took out a small delicate gold-chased lighter. It was a woman's lighter and it had an initial on it in diamonds— the letter C. "It wouldn't be your wife's, would it?"

"Not with the initial C. No, it's not Ellie's," I said. "She hadn't anything of that kind. And it's not Miss Andersen's either. Her name is Greta."

"It was up there where somebody had dropped it. It's a classy bits of goods—cost money."

"C," I said, repeating the initial thoughtfully. "I can't think of anyone who's been with us whose initial is C except Cora," I said. "That's my wife's stepmother, Mrs. Van Stuyvestant, but I really can't see her scrambling up to the Folly along that very overgrown path. And anyway, she hasn't been staying with us for quite a long time. About a month. I don't think I've ever seen her using this lighter. Perhaps I wouldn't notice anyway," I said. "Miss Andersen might know."

"Well, take it up with you and show it to her."

"I will. But if so, if it's Cora's, it seems odd that we've never seen it when we've been in the Folly lately. There's not much stuff there. You'd notice something like this lying on the floor—it was on the floor?"

"Yes, quite near the divan. Of course anybody might use that Folly. It's a handy place, you know, for a couple of lovers to meet any time. The locals I'm talking about. But they wouldn't be likely to have a thing of this kind."

"There's Claudia Hardcastle," I said, "but I doubt if she'd have anything as fancy as this. And what would she be doing in the Folly?"

"She's quite a friend of your wife's, isn't she?"

"Yes," I said, "I think she's Ellie's best friend down here."

"Ah," said Sergeant Keene.

I looked at him rather hard. "You don't think Claudia Hardcastle was a—an enemy of Ellie's, do you? That would be absurd."

"Doesn't seem any reason why she should be, I agree, but you never know with ladies."

"I suppose—" I began, and then stopped because what I was going to say would seem perhaps rather odd.

"Yes, Mr. Rogers?"

"I believe that Claudia Hardcastle was originally married to an American—an American named Lloyd. Actually that's the name of my wife's principal trustee in America—Stanford Lloyd. But there must be hundreds of Lloyds and anyway, it would only be a coincidence if it was the same person. And what would it have to do with all this?"

"It doesn't seem likely. But then—" he stopped.

"The funny thing is that I thought I saw Stanford Lloyd down here on the day of—the accident—having lunch in the George at Bartington—"

"He didn't come to see you?"

I shook my head.

"He was with someone who looked rather like Miss Hardcastle. But probably it was just a mistake on my part. You know, I suppose, that it was her brother who built our house?"

"Does she take an interest in the house?"

"No," I said, "I don't think she likes her brother's type of architecture." Then I got up. "Well, I won't take any more of your time. Try and find the gipsy."

"We shan't stop looking, I can tell you that. Coroner wants her, too."

I said good-by and went out of the police station. In the queer way that so often happens when you suddenly meet someone you've been talking about, Claudia Hardcastle came out of the post office just as I was passing it. We both stopped. She said with that slight embarrassment that you have when you meet someone that's been recently bereaved,

"I'm so terribly sorry, Mike, about Ellie. I won't say any more. It's beastly when people say things to you. But I have just—just to say that."

"I know," I said. "You were very nice to Ellie. You made her feel at home here. I've been grateful."

"There was one thing I wanted to ask you and I thought perhaps I'd better do it now before you go to America. I hear you're going quite soon."

"As soon as I can. I've got a lot to see to there."

"It was only—if you were putting your house on the market, I thought it might be a thing you'd set in motion before you went away. . . . And if so—if so, I'd rather like to have the first refusal of it."

I stared at her. This really did surprise me. It was the last thing I'd expected.

"You mean you'd like to buy it? I thought you didn't even care for that type of architecture?"

"My brother Rudolf said to me that it was the best thing he'd done. I daresay he knows. I expect you'll want a very large price for it, but I could pay it. Yes, I'd like to have it."

I couldn't help thinking it was odd. She'd never shown the faintest appreciation of our house when she'd come to it. I wondered as I'd wondered once or twice before what her links with her half-brother really were. Had she really a great devotion to him? Sometimes I'd almost thought that she disliked him, perhaps hated him. She spoke of him certainly in a very odd way. But whatever her actual emotions were, he meant something to her—meant something important. I shook my head slowly.

"I can see that you might think I'd want to sell the place and leave here because of Ellie's death," I said. "But actually that's not so at all. We lived here and were happy, and this is the place I shall remember her best. I shan't sell Gipsy's Acre—not for any consideration! You can be quite sure of that."

Our eyes met. It was like a kind of tussle between us. Then hers dropped.

I took my courage in both hands and spoke.

"It's no business of mine, but you were married once. Was the name of your husband Stanford Lloyd?"

She looked at me for a moment without speaking. Then she said abruptly,

"Yes," and turned away.

21

Confusion— That's all I can remember when I look back. Newspapermen asking questions—wanting interviews —masses of letters and telegrams—Greta coping with them—

The first really startling thing was that Ellie's family were not, as we had supposed, in America. It was quite a shock to find that most of them were actually in England. It was understandable, perhaps, that Cora van Stuyvesant should be. She was a very restless woman, always dashing across to Europe—to Italy, to Paris, to London and back again to America—to Palm Beach, out West to the ranch; here, there and everywhere. On the actual day of Ellie's death she had been not more than fifty miles away, still pursuing her whim of having a house in England. She had rushed over to stay in London for two or three days and gone to fresh house agents for fresh orders to view and had been touring round the country seeing half a dozen on that particular day.

Stanford Lloyd, it turned out, had flown over in the same plane for a business meeting in London. These people learned of Ellie's death, not from the cables which we had dispatched to the United States, but from the public press.

An ugly wrangle developed about where Ellie should be buried. I had assumed it was only natural that she'd be buried here where she had died—here where she and I had lived.

But Ellie's family objected violently to this. They wanted the body in due course brought to America to be buried with her forebears—where her grandfather and her father, her mother and others had been laid to rest. I suppose it was natural, really, when one comes to think of it.

Andrew Lippincott came down to talk to me about it. He put the matter in a reasonable way.

"She never left any directions as to where she wished to be buried," he pointed out to me.

"Why should she?" I demanded hotly. "How old was she—twenty-one? You don't think at twenty-one you're going to die. You don't start thinking then the way you want to be buried. If we'd ever thought about it, we'd assume we'd be buried together somewhere even if we didn't die at the same time. But who thinks of death in the middle of life?"

"A very just observation," said Mr. Lippincott. Then he said, "I'm afraid you'll also have to come to America, you know. There's a great deal of business interests you'll have to look into."

"What sort of business? What have I got to do with business?"

"You could have a great deal to do with it," he said. "Don't you realize that you're the principal beneficiary under the will?"

"You mean because I'm Ellie's next of kin or something?"

"No. Under her will."

"I didn't know she ever made a will."

"Oh, yes," said Mr. Lippincott. "Ellie was quite a businesslike young woman. She'd had to be, you know. She'd lived in the middle of that kind of thing. She made a will on coming of age and almost immediately after she was married. It was lodged with her lawyer in London with a request that one copy should be sent to me." He hesitated and then said, "If you do come to the States, which I advise, I also think that you should place your affairs in the hands of some reputable lawyer there."

"Why?"

"Because in the case of a vast fortune, large quantities of real estate, stocks, controlling interests in varying industries, you will need technical advice."

"I'm not qualified to deal with things like that," I said. "Really, I'm not."

"I quite understand," said Mr. Lippincott.

"Couldn't I place the whole thing in your hands?"

"You could do so."

"Well, then, why don't I?"

"All the same, I think you should be separately represented. I am already acting for some members of the family, and a conflict of interests might arise. If you will leave it in my hands, I will see that your interests are safeguarded by your being represented by a thoroughly able attorney."

"Thank you," I said, "you're very kind."

"If I may be slightly indiscreet—" he looked a little uncomfortable—it pleased me rather thinking of Lippincott being indiscreet.

"Yes?" I said.

"I should advise you to be very careful of anything you sign. Any business documents. Before you sign anything, read it thoroughly and carefully."

"Would the kind of document you're talking about mean anything to me if I do read it?"

"If it is not all clear to you, you will then hand it over to your legal adviser."

"Are you warning me against somebody or someone?" I said, with a suddenly aroused interest.

"That is not at all a proper question for me to answer," said Mr. Lippincott. "I will go this far. Where large sums of money are concerned, it is advisable to trust nobody."

So he was warning me against someone, but he wasn't going to give me any names. I could see that. Was it against Cora? Or had he had suspicions—perhaps suspicions of some long standing—of Stanford Lloyd, that florid banker so full of bonhomie, so rich and carefree, who had recently been over here "on business"? Might it be Uncle Frank who might approach me with some plausible documents? I had a sudden vision of myself, a poor innocent boob, swimming in a lake surrounded by evilly disposed crocodiles, all smiling false smiles of amity.

"The world," said Mr. Lippincott, "is a very evil place."

It was perhaps a stupid thing to say, but quite suddenly I asked him a question.

"Does Ellie's death benefit anyone?" I asked.

He looked at me sharply.

"That's a very curious question. Why do you ask that?"

"I don't know," I said, "it just came into my head."

"It benefits you," he said.

"Of course," I said. "I take that for granted. I really meant—does it benefit anyone else?"

Mr. Lippincott was silent for quite a long time.

"If you mean," he said, "does Fenella's will benefit certain other people in the way of legacies, that is so in a minor degree. Some old servants, an old governess, one or two charities, but nothing of any particular moment. There's a legacy to Miss Andersen, but not a large one, for she has already, as you probably know, settled a very considerable sum on Miss Andersen."

I nodded. Ellie had told me she was doing that.

"You were her husband. She had no other near relations. But I take it that your question did not mean specifically that."

"I don't know quite what I meant by it," I said. "But somehow or other, you've succeeded, Mr. Lippincott, in making me feel suspicious—suspicious of I don't know whom or why. Only—well, suspicious. I don't understand finance," I added.

"No, that is quite apparent. Let me say only that I have no exact knowledge, no exact suspicions of any kind. At someone's death there is usually an accounting of their affairs. This may take place quickly or it may be delayed for a period of many years."

"What you really mean," I said, "is that some of the others quite likely might put a few fast ones over and ball up things generally. Get me perhaps to sign releases—whatever you call the things."

"If Fenella's affairs were not, shall we say, in the healthy state they ought to be, then—yes, possibly her premature death might be, shall we say, fortunate for someone—we will name no names—someone perhaps who could cover his traces more easily if he had a fairly simple person, if I may say so, like yourself to deal with. I will go that far, but I do not wish to speak further on the matter. It would not be equitable to do so."

There was a simple funeral service held in the little church. If I could have stayed away, I would have done so. I hated all those people who were staring at me lining up outside the church. Curious eyes. Greta pulled me through things. I don't think I'd realized until now what a strong, reliable character she was. She made the arrangements, ordered flowers, arranged everything. I understood better now how Ellie had come to depend upon Greta as she had done. There aren't many Gretas in the world.

The people in the church were mostly our neighbors—some, even, that we had hardly known. But I noticed one face that I had seen before, but which I could not at the moment place. When I got back to the house, Carson told me there was someone in the drawing room waiting to see me.

"I can't see anyone today. Send him away. You shouldn't have let him in!"

"Excuse me, sir. He said he was a relation."

"A relation?"

Suddenly I remembered the man I'd seen in the church. Carson was handing me a card.

It meant nothing to me for a moment. Mr. William R. Pardoe. I turned it over and shook my head. Then I handed it to Greta.

"Do you know by any chance who this is?" I said. "His face seemed familiar, but I couldn't place it. Perhaps it's one of Ellie's friends."

Greta took it from me and looked at it. Then she said,

"Of course."

"Who is it?"

"Uncle Reuben. You remember. Ellie's cousin. She's spoken of him to you, surely?"

I remembered then why the face had seemed familiar to me. Ellie had had several photographs in her sitting room of her various relations carelessly placed about the room. That was why the face had been familiar to me. I had seen it so far only in a photograph.

"I'll come," I said.

I went out of the room and into the drawing room. Mr. Pardoe rose to his feet and said,

"Michael Rogers? You may not know my name, but your wife was my cousin. She called me Uncle Reuben always, but we haven't met, I know. This is the first time I've been over since your marriage."

"Of course I know who you are," I said.

I don't know quite how to describe Reuben Pardoe. He was a big burly man with a large face, wide and rather absent-looking, as though he were thinking of something else. Yet after you talked to him for a few moments, you got the feeling that he was more on the ball than you would have thought.

"I don't need to tell you how shocked and grieved I was to hear of Ellie's death," he said.

"Let's skip that," I said. "I'm not up to talking about it."

"No, no, I can understand that."

He had a certain sympathetic personality and yet there was something about him that made me vaguely uneasy. I said, as Greta entered,

"You know Miss Andersen?"

"Of course," he said. "How are you, Greta?"

"Not too bad," said Greta. "How long have you been over?"

"Just a week or two. Touring around."

"I have seen you before," I said. On an impulse I went on. "I saw you the other day."

"Really? Where?"

"At an auction sale at a place called Bartington Manor."

"I remember now," he said, "yes, yes, I think I remember your face. You were with a man about sixty with a brown mustache."

"Yes," I said. "A Major Phillpot."

"You seemed in good spirits," he said, "both of you."

"Never better," I said, and repeated with the strange wonder that I always felt, "Never better."

"Of course—at that time you didn't know what had happened. That was the date of the accident, wasn't it?"

"We were expecting," I said, "Ellie to join us for lunch."

"Tragic," said Uncle Reuben. "Really tragic . . ."

"I had no idea," I said, "that you were in England. I don't think Ellie had any idea either?" I paused, waiting for what he would tell me.

"No," he said, "I hadn't written. In fact, I didn't know how much time I should have over here, but actually I'd concluded my business earlier than I thought and I was wondering if after the sale I'd have the time to drive over and see you."

"You came over from the States on business?" I asked.

"Well, partly yes and partly no. Cora wanted some advice from me on one or two matters. One concerning this house she's thinking of buying."

It was then that he told me that Cora was in England. Again I said,

"We didn't know that even."

"She was actually staying not far from here that day," he said.

"Near here? Was she in a hotel?"

"No. she was staying with a friend."

"I didn't know she had any friends in this part of the world."

"A woman called—now what was her name?—Hard-something. Hardcastle."

"Claudia Hardcastle?" I was surprised.

"Yes. She was quite a friend of Cora's. Cora knew her when she was in the States. Didn't you know?"

"I know very little," I said. "Very little about the family."

I looked at Greta.

"Did you know that Cora knew Claudia Hardcastle?"

"I don't think I ever heard her speak of her," said Greta. "So that's why Claudia didn't turn up that day."

"Of course," I said, "she was going with you by train to London. You were to meet at Market Chadwell station—"

"Yes—and she wasn't there. She rang up the house just after I'd left. Said some American visitor was turning up unexpectedly and she couldn't leave home."

"I wonder," I said, "if the American visitor could have been Cora."

"Obviously," said Reuben Pardoe. He shook his head. "It all seems so confused," he said. He went on, "I understand the inquest was adjourned."

"Yes," I said.

He drained his cup and got up.

"I won't stay to worry you any more," he said. "If there's anything I can do, I'm staying at the Majestic Hotel in Market Chadwell."

I said I was afraid there wasn't anything he could do, and thanked him. When he had gone away, Greta said,

"What does he want, I wonder? Why did he come over?" And then sharply, "I wish they'd all go back where they belong."

22

There was nothing more for me to do at Gipsy's Acre. I left Greta in charge of the house while I sailed to New York to wind up things there and to take part in what I felt with some dread was going to be the most ghastly gold-plated obsequies for Ellie.

"You're going into the jungle," Greta warned me. "Look after yourself. Don't let them skin you alive."

She was right about that. It was the jungle. I felt it when I got there. I didn't know about jungles—not that kind of jungle. I was out of my depth, and I knew it. I wasn't the hunter; I was the hunted. There were people all around me in the undergrowth gunning for me. Sometimes, I expect, I imagined things. Sometimes my suspicions were justified. I remember going to the lawyer supplied for me by Mr. Lippincott (a most urbane man who treated me rather as a general practitioner might have done in the medical profession). I had been advised to get rid of certain mining properties to which the title deeds were not too clear.

He asked me who had told me so, and I said it was Stanford Lloyd.

"Well, we must look into it," he said. "A man like Mr. Lloyd ought to know."

He said to me afterward,

"There's nothing wrong with your title deeds, and there is certainly no point in your selling the land in a hurry, as he seems to have advised you. Hang on to it."

I had the feeling then that I'd been right—everybody was gunning for me. They all knew I was a simpleton when it came to finance.

The funeral was splendid and, I thought, quite horrible. Gold-plated, as I had surmised. At the cemetery, masses of flowers, the cemetery itself like a public park and all the trimmings of wealthy mourning expressed in monumental marble. Ellie would have hated it, I was sure of that. But I suppose her family had a certain right to her.

Four days after my arrival in New York, I had news from Kingston Bishop.

The body of old Mrs. Lee had been found in the disused quarry on the far side of the hill. She had been dead some days. There had been accidents there before, and it had been said that the place ought to be fenced in—but nothing had been done. A verdict of accidental death had been brought in, and a further recommendation to the council to fence the place off. In Mrs. Lee's cottage a sum of three hundred pounds had been found hidden under the floor boards, all in one-pound notes.

Major Phillpot had added in a postscript, "I'm sure you will be sorry to hear that Claudia Hardcastle was thrown from her horse and killed out hunting yesterday."

Claudia—killed? I couldn't believe it! It gave me a very nasty jolt. Two people—within a fortnight, killed in a riding accident. It seemed like an almost impossible coincidence.

I don't want to dwell on that time I spent in New York. I was a stranger in an alien atmosphere. I felt all the time that I had to be wary of what I said and what I did. The Ellie that I had known, the Ellie had had belonged peculiarly to me, was not there. I saw her now only as an American girl, heiress to a great fortune, surrounded by friends and connections and distant relatives, one of a family that had lived there for five generations. She had come from there as a comet might have come, visiting my territory.

Now she had gone back to be buried with her own folk, to where her own home was. I was glad to have it that way. I shouldn't have been easy feeling her there in the prim little cemetery at the foot of the pine woods just outside the village. No, I shouldn't have been easy.

"Go back where you belong, Ellie," I said to myself.

Now and again that haunting little tune of the song she used to sing to her guitar came into my mind. I remembered her fingers gently twanging the strings.

> Every Morn and every Night
> Some are born to Sweet Delight

and I thought, "That was true of you. You were born to Sweet Delight. You had Sweet Delight there at Gipsy's Acre. Only it didn't last very long. Now it's over. You've come back to where perhaps there wasn't much delight, where you weren't happy. But you're at home here, anyway. You're among your own folk."

I wondered suddenly where I should be when the time came for me to die. Gipsy's Acre? It could be. My mother would come and see me laid in my grave—if she wasn't dead already. But I couldn't think of my mother being dead. I could think more easily of death for myself. Yes, she'd come and see me buried. Perhaps the sternness of her face wouldn't relax. I took my thoughts away from her. I didn't want to think of her. I didn't want to go near her or see her.

That last isn't quite true. It wasn't a question of seeing her. It was always with my mother a question of her seeing me, of her eyes looking through me, of an anxiety that swept out like a miasma embracing me. I thought, "Mothers are the devil! Why have they got to brood over their children? Why do they feel they know all about their children? They don't. They don't! She ought to be proud of me, happy for me, happy for the wonderful life that I've achieved. She ought—" Then I wrenched my thoughts away from her again.

How long was I over in the States? I can't even remember. It seemed an age of walking warily, of being watched by people with false smiles and enmity in their eyes. I said to myself every day, "I've got to get through this. I've got to get through this—and then—" Those were the two words I used. Used in my own mind, I mean. I used them every day several times. And then— They were the two words of the future. I used them in the same way that I had once used those other two words—I want . . .

Everyone went out of their way to be nice to me because I was rich! Under the terms of Ellie's will, I was an extremely rich man. It felt very odd. I had investments I didn't understand—shares, stocks, property. And I didn't know in the least what to do with them all.

The day before I went back to England, I had a long conversation with Mr. Lippincott. I always thought of him like that in my mind—as Mr. Lippincott. He'd never become Uncle Andrew to me. I told him that I thought of withdrawing the charge of my investments from Stanford Lloyd.

"Indeed!" His grizzled eyebrows rose. He looked at me with his shrewd eyes and his poker face and I wondered what exactly his "indeed" meant.

"Do you think it's all right to do that?" I asked anxiously.

"You have reasons, I presume?"

"No," I said, "I haven't got reasons. A feeling, that's all. I suppose I can say anything to you?"

"The communication will be privileged, naturally."

"All right," I said. "I just feel that he's a crook!"

"Ah." Mr. Lippincott looked interested. "Yes, I should say your instinct was possibly sound."

So I knew then that I was right. Stanford Lloyd had been playing hanky-panky with Ellie's bonds and investments and all the rest of it. I signed a power of attorney and gave it to Andrew Lippincott.

"You're willing," I said, "to accept it?"

"As far as financial matters are concerned," said Mr. Lippincott, "you can trust me absolutely. I will do my best for you in that respect. I don't think you will have any reason to complain of my stewardship."

I wondered exactly what he meant by that. He meant something. I think he meant that he didn't like me, had never liked me, but financially he would do his best for me because I had been Ellie's husband. I signed all necessary papers. He asked me how I was going back to England. Flying? I said no, I wasn't flying, I was going by sea. "I've got to have a little time to myself," I said. "I think a sea voyage will do me good."

"And you are going back to take up your residence—where?"

"Gipsy's Acre," I said.

"Ah. You propose to live there."

"Yes," I said.

"I thought perhaps you might have put it on the market for sale."

"No," I said, and the no came out rather stronger than I

meant. I wasn't going to part with Gipsy's Acre. Gipsy's Acre had been part of my dream—the dream that I'd cherished since I'd been a callow boy.

"Is anybody looking after it while you have been away in the States?"

I said that I'd left Greta Andersen in charge.

"Ah," said Mr. Lippincott, "yes. Greta."

He meant something in the way he said "Greta" but I didn't take him up on it. If he disliked her, he disliked her. He always had. It left an awkward pause, then I changed my mind. I felt that I'd got to say something.

"She was very good to Ellie," I said. "She nursed her when she was ill. She came and lived with us and looked after Ellie. I—I can't be grateful enough to her. I'd like you to understand that. You don't know what she's been like. You don't know how she helped and did everything after Ellie was killed. I don't know what I'd have done without her."

"Quite so, quite so," said Mr. Lippincott. He sounded drier than you could possibly imagine.

"So you see I owe her a lot."

"A very competent girl," said Mr. Lippincott.

I got up and said good-by and I thanked him.

"You have nothing for which to thank me," said Mr. Lippincott, dry as ever.

He added, "I wrote you a short letter. I have sent it by air mail to Gipsy's Acre. If you are going by sea, you will probably find it waiting there on arrival." Then he said, "Have a good voyage."

So that was that.

When I got back to my hotel, I found a cable. It asked me to come to a hospital in California. It said a friend of mine, Rudolf Santonix, had asked for me, he had not long to live and he wished to see me before he died.

I changed my passage to a later boat and flew to San Francisco. He wasn't dead yet, but he was sinking very fast. They doubted, they said, if he would recover consciousness before he died, but he had asked for me very urgently. I sat there in that hospital room watching him, watching what looked like a shell of the man I knew. He'd always looked ill, he'd always had a kind of queer transparency about him, a delicacy, a frailness. He lay now looking a deadly, waxen figure. I sat there thinking, "I wish he'd speak to me. I wish he'd say something. Just something before he dies."

I felt so alone, so horribly alone. I'd escaped from enemies now, I'd got to a friend—my only friend, really. He was the only person who knew anything about me, except Mum, but I didn't want to think of Mum.

Once or twice I spoke to a nurse, asked her if there wasn't anything they could do, but she shook her head and said noncommittally,

"He might recover consciousness or might not."

I sat there. And then at last he stirred and sighed. The nurse raised him up very gently. He looked at me but I didn't know whether he recognized me or not. He was just looking at me as though he looked past me and beyond me. Then suddenly a difference came into his eyes. I thought, "He does know me; he does see me." He said something very faintly, and I bent over the bed so as to catch it. But they didn't seem words that had any meaning. Then his body had a sudden spasm and twitch, and he threw his head back and shouted out,

"You damned fool. . . . Why didn't you go the other way?"

Then he just collapsed and died.

I don't know what he meant—or even if he knew himself what he was saying.

So that was the last I saw of Santonix. I wonder if he'd have heard me if I had said anything to him? I'd like to have told him once more that the house he'd built me was the best thing I had in the world—the thing that mattered most to me. Funny that a house could mean that. I suppose it was a sort of symbolism about it. Something you want. Something you want so much that you don't quite know what it is. But he'd known what it was and he'd given it to me. And I'd got it. And I was going home to it.

Going home. That's all I could think about when I got on the boat—that and a deadly tiredness at first. . . .

And then a rising tide of happiness oozing up, as it were, from the depths. . . . I was going home. I was going home . . .

> Home is the sailor, home from the sea
> And the hunter home from the hill . . .

23

Yes, that was what I was doing. It was all over now. The last of the fight, the last of the struggle. The last phase of the journey.

It seemed so long ago to the time of my restless youth. The days of "I want, I want." But it wasn't long. Less than a year. . . .

I went over it all— lying there in my bunk and thinking.

Meeting Ellie—our times in Regent's Park—our marriage in the registrar's office. The house—Santonix building it—the house completed. Mine, all mine. I was me —me—me as I wanted to be—as I'd always wanted to be. I'd got everything I'd wanted, and I was going home to it.

Before I left New York, I'd written one letter and sent it off by air mail to get there ahead of me. I'd written to Phillpot. Somehow I felt that Phillpot would understand, though others mightn't.

It was easier to write than to tell him. Anyway, he'd got to know. Everyone had got to know. Some people probably wouldn't understand, but I thought he would. He'd seen for himself how close Ellie and Greta had been, how Ellie had depended upon Greta. I thought he'd realize how I'd come to depend upon her also, how it would be impossible for me to live alone in the house where I'd lived with Ellie unless there was someone there to help me. I don't know if I put it very well. I did my best.

"I'd like you," I wrote, "to be the first one to know. You've been so kind to us, and I think you'll be the only person to understand. I can't face living all alone at Gipsy's Acre. I've been thinking all the time I've been in America and I've decided that as soon as I get home, I'm going to ask Greta to marry me. She's the only person I can really talk to about Ellie, you see. She'll understand. Perhaps she won't marry me, but I think she will. . . . It will make everything as though there were the three of us together still."

I wrote the letter three times before I could get it to express just what I wanted to say. Phillpot ought to get it two days before my return.

I came up on deck as we were approaching England. I looked out as the land came nearer. I thought, "I wish Santonix was with me." I did wish it. I wished he could know how everything was all coming true—everything I'd planned—everything I'd thought—everything I'd wanted.

I'd shaken off America, I'd shaken off the crooks and the sycophants and all the whole lot of them whom I hated and whom I was pretty sure hated me and looked down on me for being so low-class! I was coming back in triumph. I was coming back to the pine trees and the curling, dangerous road that made its way up through Gipsy's Acre to the house on the hilltop. My house! I was coming back to the two things I wanted. My house—the house that I'd dreamed of, that I'd planned, that I'd wanted above everything. That and a wonderful woman. . . . I'd known always that I'd meet one day a wonderful woman. I had met her. I'd seen her and she'd seen me. We'd come together. A wonderful woman. I'd known the moment I saw her that I belonged to her, belonged to her absolutely and for always. I was hers. And now—at last—I was going to her.

Nobody saw me arrive at Kingston Bishop. It was almost dark and I came by train and I walked from the station, taking a roundabout side road. I didn't want to meet any of the people of the village. Not that night. . . .

The sun had set when I came up the road to Gipsy's Acre. I'd told Greta the time I'd arrive. She was up there in the house waiting for me. At last! We'd done with sub-terfuges now and all the pretenses—the pretense of dislik-ing her— I thought now, laughing to myself, of the part I'd played, a part I'd played carefully right from the be-ginning. Disliking Greta, not wanting her to come and stay with Ellie. Yes, I'd been very careful. Everyone must have been taken in by that pretense. I remembered the quarrel we'd faked up so that Ellie should overhear it.

Greta had known me for what I was the first moment we met. We'd never had any silly illusions about each other. She had the same kind of mind, the same kind of desires as I had. We wanted the world, nothing less! We wanted to be on top of the world. We wanted to fulfill every ambition. We wanted to have everything, deny our-selves nothing. I remembered how I'd poured out my heart to her when I first met her in Hamburg, telling my frenzied desire for things. I hadn't got to conceal my in-ordinate greed for life from Greta. She has the same greed herself. She said,

"For all you want out of life, you've got to have money."

"Yes," I said, "and I don't see how I'm going to get it."

"No," said Greta, "you won't get it by hard work. You're not the kind."

"Work!" I said. "I'd have to work for years! I don't want to wait. I don't want to be middle-aged." I said, "You know the story about that chap Schliemann, how he worked, toiled, and made a fortune so that he could have his life's dream come true and go to Troy and dig it up and find the graves of Troy. He got his dream, but he had to wait until he was forty. But I don't want to wait till I'm a middle-aged man. Old. One foot in the grave. I want it now when I'm young and strong. You do too, don't you?" I said.

"Yes. And I know the way you can do it. It's easy. I wonder you haven't thought of it already. You can get girls easily enough, can't you? I can see that. I can feel it."

"Do you think I care about girls—or ever have really? There's only one girl I want," I said. "You. And you know that. I belong to you. I knew it the moment I saw you. I knew always that I'd meet someone like you. And I have. I belong to you."

"Yes," said Greta, "I think you do."

"We both want the same things out of life," I said.

"I tell you it's easy," said Greta. "Easy. All you've got to do is to marry a rich girl—one of the richest girls in the world. I can put you in the way of doing that."

"Don't be fantastic," I said.

"It's not fantastic; it'll be easy."

"No," I said, "that's no good to me. I don't want to be the husband of a rich wife. She'll buy me things and we'll do things and she'll keep me in a golden cage, but that's not what I want. I don't want to be a tied-up slave."

"You needn't be. It's the sort of thing that needn't last for long. Just long enough. Wives do die, you know."

I stared at her.

"Now you're shocked," she said.

"No," I said, "I'm not shocked."

"I thought you wouldn't be. I thought perhaps already—?" She looked at me inquiringly, but I wasn't going to answer that. I had still some self-preservation left. There are some secrets one doesn't want anyone to know. Not that they were much in the way of secrets, but I didn't like to think of them. I didn't like to think of the first one. Silly, though. Puerile. Nothing that mattered. I had had a boy's passion for a classy wrist watch that a boy—a friend of mine at school—had been given. I wanted it. I wanted it badly. It had cost a lot of money. A rich godfather had given it to him. Yes, I wanted that, but I didn't think I'd ever have a chance of getting it. Then there was the day we went skating together. The ice wasn't strong enough to bear. Not that we thought of it beforehand. It just happened. The ice cracked. I skated across to him. He was hanging on. He had gone through a hole and he was hanging onto the ice which was cutting his hands. I went across to pull him out, of course, but just as I got there, I saw the glint of the wrist watch. I thought, "Supposing he goes under and drowns." I thought how easy it would be. . . .

It seemed almost unconsciously, I think, that I unfastened the strap, grabbed the watch and pushed his head under instead of trying to pull him out. . . . Just held his head under. He couldn't struggle much; he was under the ice. People saw and came toward us. They thought I was trying to pull him out! They got him out in due course, with some difficulty. They tried artificial respiration on him, but it was too late. I hid my treasure away in a special place where I kept things now and then—things I didn't want Mum to see because she'd ask me where I got them. She came across that watch one day when she was fooling about with my socks. Asked me if that wasn't Pete's watch? I said of course it wasn't—it was one I'd swapped with a boy at school.

I was always nervous with Mum—I always felt she knew too much about me. I was nervous with her when she found the watch. She suspected, I think. She couldn't know, of course. Nobody knew. But she used to look at me—in a funny way. Everybody thought I'd tried to rescue Pete. I don't think she ever thought so. I think she knew. She didn't want to know, but her trouble was that she knew too much about me. I felt a bit guilty myself sometimes, but it wore off fairly soon.

And then later on, when I was in camp—it was during our military training time—chap called Ed and I had been to a sort of gambling place. I'd had no luck at all, lost everything I had, but Ed had won a packet. He changed his chips, and he and I were coming home and he was stuffed up with notes. His pockets were bulged with them. Then a couple of toughs came round the corner and went for us. They were pretty handy with the flick knives they'd got. I got a cut in the arm, but Ed got a proper sort of stab. He went down under it. Then there was a noise of people coming. The toughs hooked it. I could see that if I was quick . . . I was quick! My reflexes are pretty good —I wrapped a handkerchief round my hand and I pulled out the knife from Ed's wound and I stuck the knife in again a couple of times in better places. He gave a gasp and passed out. I was scared, of course—scared for a second or two, and then I knew it was going to be all right. So I felt—well—naturally I felt proud of myself for thinking and acting quick! I thought, "Poor old Ed; he always was a fool." It took me no time at all to transfer those notes to my own pocket! Nothing like having quick reflexes, seizing your opportunity. The trouble is the opportunities don't come very often. Some people, I suppose, get scared when they know they've killed someone. But I wasn't scared. Not this time.

Mind you, it's not a thing you want to do too often. Not unless it might be really worth your while. I don't know how Greta sensed that about me. But she'd known. I don't mean that she'd known that I'd actually killed a couple of people. But I think she knew the idea of killing wouldn't shock me or upset me. I said,

"What's all this fantastic story, Greta?"

She said, "I am in a position to help you. I can bring you in touch with one of the richest girls in America. I more or less look after her. I live with her. I have a lot of influence over her."

"Do you think she'd look at someone like me?" I said. I didn't believe it for a moment. Why should a rich girl, who could have her pick of any attractive, sexy man she liked, go for me?

"You've got a lot of sex appeal," said Greta. "Girls go for you, don't they?"

I grinned and said I didn't do too badly.

"She's never had that kind of thing. She's been looked after too well. The only young men she's been allowed to meet are conventional kinds—bankers' sons, tycoons' sons. She's groomed to make a good marriage in the moneyed class. They're terrified of her meeting handsome foreigners who might be after her money. But naturally she's keener on people like that. They'd be new to her, something she's never seen before. You've got to make a big play for her. You've got to fall in love with her at first sight and sweep her off her feet! It'll be easy enough. She's never had anyone to make a real sexy approach to her. You could do it."

"I could try," I said doubtfully.

"We could set it up," said Greta.

"Her family would step in and stop it."

"No, they wouldn't," said Greta. "They wouldn't

know anything about it. Not until it was too late. Not until you'd got married secretly."

"So that's your idea?"

So we talked about it. We planned. Not in detail, mind you. Greta went back to America, but she kept in touch with me. I went on with various jobs. I'd told her about Gipsy's Acre and that I wanted it, and she said that was just fine for setting up a romantic story. We laid our plans so that my meeting with Ellie would take place there. Greta would work Ellie up about having a house in England and getting away from her family as soon as she came of age.

Oh, yes, we set it up. Greta was a great planner. I don't think I could have planned it, but I knew I could play my part all right. I'd always enjoyed playing a part. And so that's how it happened. That's how I met Ellie.

It was fun, all of it. Mad fun because, of course, there was always a risk—there was always a danger that it wouldn't come off. The thing that made me really nervous were the times that I had to meet Greta. I had to be sure, you see, that I never gave myself away by looking at Greta. I tried not to look at her. We agreed it was best that I should take a dislike to her, pretend jealousy of her. I carried that out all right. I remember the day she came down to stay. We staged a quarrel—a quarrel that Ellie could hear. I don't know whether we overdid it a bit. I don't think so. Sometimes I was nervous that Ellie might guess or something, but I don't think she did. I don't know. I don't know, really. I never did know about Ellie.

It was very easy to make love to Ellie. She was very sweet. Yes, she was really sweet. Just sometimes I was afraid of her because she did things without telling me. And she knew things that I never dreamt she knew. But she loved me. Yes, she loved me. Sometimes—I think I loved her too. . . .

I don't mean it was ever like Greta. Greta was the woman I belonged to. She was sex personified. I was mad for her, and I had to hold myself in. Ellie was something different. I enjoyed living with her, you know. Yes, that sounds very queer now I think back to it. I enjoyed living with her very much.

I'm putting this down now because this is what I was thinking that evening when I arrived back from America. When I arrived back on top of the world, having got all I'd longed for in spite of the risks, in spite of the dangers, in spite of having done a pretty good murder, though I say it myself!

Yes, it was a bit tricky, I thought once or twice, but nobody could tell, not the way we'd done it. Now the risks were over, the dangers were over, and here I was coming up to Gipsy's Acre—coming as I'd come up it that day after I'd first seen the poster on the walls and gone up to look at the ruins of the old house. Coming up and rounding the bend—

And then—it was then I saw her. I mean it was then I saw Ellie. Just as I came round the corner of the road in the dangerous place where the accidents happened. She was there in the same place just where she'd been before, standing in the shadow of the fir tree. Just as she'd stood, when she'd started a little as she saw me and I'd started, seeing her. There we'd looked at each other first and I'd come up and spoken to her, played the part of the young man who's fallen suddenly in love. Played it jolly well, too! Oh, I tell you I'm a fine actor!

But I hadn't expected to see her now. . . . I mean, I couldn't see her now, could I? But I was seeing her. . . . She was looking—looking straight at me. Only—there was something that frightened me—something that frightened me very much. It was, you see, just as though she didn't see me—I mean I knew she couldn't really be there. I knew she was dead—but I saw her. She was dead and her body was buried in the cemetery in the U.S.A. But all the same, she was standing under the fir tree and she was looking at me. No, not at me. She was looking as though she expected to see me, and there was love in her face— the same love that I had seen one day—one day when she'd been plucking the strings of her guitar—that day when she'd said to me, "What were you thinking of?" and I said, "Why do you ask me?" and she said, "You were looking at me as though you loved me." I'd said something silly like "Of course I love you."

I stopped dead. I stopped dead there in the road. I was shaking. I said out loud,

"Ellie."

She didn't move; she just stayed there looking . . . looking straight through me. That's what frightened me because I knew if I thought for a minute, I'd know why she didn't see me, and I didn't want to know. No, I didn't want to know that. I was quite sure that I didn't want to know that. Looking straight at the place where I was—not seeing me. I ran then. I ran like a coward up the rest of the road to where the lights were shining in my house, until I pulled myself out of the silly panic that I was in. This was my triumph. I'd got home. I was the hunter home from the hills, back to my house, back to the other thing that I'd wanted more than anything in the world, to the wonderful woman whom I belonged to body and soul.

And now we'd get married and we'd live in the House. We'd get all we'd played for! We'd won— Won hands down!

The door wasn't latched. I went in, stamping my feet, and through the open door of the library. And there was Greta standing by the window waiting for me. She was glorious. She was the most glorious and the most lovely thing I'd ever seen. She was like a Brunnehilde, a super Valkyrie with shining golden hair. She smelt and looked and tasted of sex. We'd denied ourselves so long except for occasional brief meetings up in the Folly.

I came straight into her arms, a sailor home from the sea to where he belonged. Yes, it was one of the most wonderful moments of my life.

Presently we came down to earth. I sat down and she shoved a small pile of letters toward me. I picked out almost automatically one with an American stamp. It was the air mail letter from Lippincott. I wondered what he'd put in it, why he'd had to write me a letter?

"Well," said Greta with a deep, satisfied sigh, "we've made it."

"V-day all right," I said.

We both laughed, laughed wildly. There was champagne on the table. I opened it and we drank to each other.

"This place is wonderful," I said, looking round. "It's more beautiful than I remember it. Santonix— But I haven't told you. Santonix is dead."

"Oh, dear," said Greta, "what a pity. So he really was ill?"

"Of course he was ill. I never wanted to think so. I went and saw him when he was dying."

Greta gave a little shiver.

"I shouldn't like to do that. Did he say anything?"

"Not really. He said I was a damned fool—I ought to have gone the other way."

"What did he mean—what way?"

"I don't know what he meant," I said. "I suppose he was delirious. Didn't know what he was talking about."

"Well, this house is a fine monument to his memory," said Greta. "I think we'll stick on to it, don't you?"

I stared at her. "Of course. Do you think I'm going to live anywhere else?"

"We can't live here all the time," said Greta. "Not all the year round. Buried in a hole like this village?"

"But it's where I want to live—it's where I always meant to live."

"Yes, of course. But after all, Mike, we've got all the money in the world. We can go anywhere! We can go all over the Continent—we'll go on safari in Africa. We'll have adventures. We'll go and look for things—exciting pictures. We'll go to the Angkor Vat. Don't you want to have an adventurous life?"

"Well, I suppose so . . . But we'll always come back here, won't we?"

I had a queer feeling—a queer feeling that something had gone wrong somewhere. That's all I'd ever thought of. My house and Greta. I hadn't wanted anything else. But she did. I saw that. She was just beginning. Beginning to want things. Beginning to know she could have them. I had a sudden cruel foreboding. I began to shiver.

"What's the matter with you, Mike? You're shivering. Have you caught a cold or something?"

"It's not that," I said.

"What's happened, Mike?"

"I saw Ellie," I said.

"What do you mean, you saw Ellie?"

"As I was walking up the road, I turned the corner and there she was, standing under a fir tree, looking at—I mean looking toward me."

Greta stared.

"Don't be ridiculous. You—you imagined things."

"Perhaps one does imagine things. This is Gipsy's Acre, after all. Ellie was there, all right, looking—looking quite happy. Just like herself, as though she'd—she'd always been there and was always going to be there."

"Mike!" Greta took hold of my shoulder. She shook me. "Mike, don't say things like that. Had you been drinking before you got here?"

"No, I waited till I got here to you. I knew you'd have champagne waiting for us."

"Well, let's forget Ellie and drink to ourselves."

"It was Ellie," I said obstinately.

"Of course it wasn't Ellie! It was just a trick of the light—something like that."

"It was Ellie, and she was standing there. She was looking—looking for me and at me. But she couldn't see me. Greta, she couldn't see me." My voice rose. "And I know why. I know why she couldn't see me."

"What do you mean?"

It was then that I whispered for the first time under my breath,

"Because that wasn't me. I wasn't there. There was nothing for her to see but Endless Night." Then I shouted out in a panic-stricken voice, "Some are born to Sweet Delight, some are born to Sweet Delight and some are born to Endless Night. Me, Greta, me.

"Do you remember, Greta," I said, "how she sat on that sofa? She used to play that song on her guitar, singing it in her gentle voice. You must remember.

"'Every Night and every Morn,'" I sang it under my

breath, " 'Some to Misery are born. Every Morn and every Night some are born to Sweet Delight.' That's Ellie, Greta. She was born to sweet delight. 'Some are born to Sweet Delight, Some are born to Endless Night.' That's what Mum knew about me. She knew I was born to endless night. I hadn't got there yet. And Santonix knew. He knew I was heading that way. But it mightn't have happened. There was just a moment, just one moment, the time Ellie sang that song. I could have been quite happy, couldn't I, really, married to Ellie? I could have gone on being married to Ellie."

"No, you couldn't," said Greta. "I never thought you were the type of person who lost your nerve, Mike." She shook me roughly by the shoulder again. "Wake up."

I stared at her.

"I'm sorry, Greta. What have I been saying?"

"I suppose they got you down over there in the States. But you did all right, didn't you? I mean, all the investments are all right?"

"Everything's fixed," I said. "Everything's fixed for our future. Our glorious, glorious future."

"You speak very queerly. I'd like to know what Lippincott says in his letter."

I pulled his letter toward me and opened it. There was nothing inside except a cutting from a paper—not a new cutting. It was old and rather rubbed. I stared down at it. It was a picture of a street. I recognized the street, with rather a grand building in the background. It was a street in Hamburg with some people coming toward the photographer—two people in the forefront walking arm in arm. They were Greta and myself. So Lippincott had known. He'd known all along that I already knew Greta. Somebody must have sent him this cutting sometime, probably with no nefarious intention. Just amused perhaps to recognize Miss Greta Andersen walking along the streets of Hamburg. He had known I knew Greta and I remembered how particularly he had asked me whether I had met or not met Greta Andersen. I had denied it, of course, but he'd known I was lying. It must have begun his suspicion of me.

173

I was suddenly afraid of Lippincott. He couldn't suspect, of course, that I'd killed Ellie. He suspected something, though. Perhaps he suspected even that.

"Look," I said to Greta, "he knew we knew each other. He's known it all along. I've always hated that old fox and he's always hated you," I said. "When he knows that we're going to marry, he'll suspect." But then I knew that Lippincott had certainly suspected that Greta and I were going to marry, he suspected that we knew each other, he suspected perhaps that we were lovers.

"Mike, will you stop being a panic-stricken rabbit. Yes, that's what I said—a panic-stricken rabbit. I admired you. I've always admired you. But now you're falling to pieces. You're afraid of everyone."

"Don't say that to me."

"Well, it's true."

"Endless night."

I couldn't think of anything else to say. I was still wondering just what it meant. Endless night. It meant blackness. It meant that I wasn't there to be seen. I could see the dead, but the dead couldn't see me although I was living. They couldn't see me because I wasn't really there. The man who loved Ellie wasn't really there. He'd entered of his own accord into endless night. I bent my head lower toward the ground.

"Endless night," I said again.

"Stop saying that," Greta screamed. "Stand up! Be a man, Mike. Don't give in to this absurd superstitious fancy."

"How can I help it?" I said. "I've sold my soul to Gipsy's Acre, haven't I? Gipsy's Acre's never been safe. It's never been safe for anyone. It wasn't safe for Ellie and it isn't safe for me. Perhaps it isn't safe for you."

"What do you mean?"

I got up. I went toward her. I loved her. Yes, I loved her still with a last tense sexual desire. But love, hate, desire—aren't they all the same? Three in one and one in three. I could never have hated Ellie, but I hated Greta. I enjoyed hating her. I hated her with all my heart and with a leaping joyous wish—I couldn't wait for the safe ways, I didn't want to wait for them. I came nearer to her.

"You filthy bitch!" I said. "You hateful, glorious, golden-haired bitch. You're not safe, Greta. You're not safe from me. Do you understand? I've learned to enjoy —to enjoy killing people. I was excited the day that I knew Ellie had gone out with that horse to her death. I enjoyed myself all the morning because of killing, but I've never got near enough to killing until now. This is different. I want more than just knowing that someone's going to die because of a capsule they swallowed at breakfast time. I want more than pushing an old woman over a quarry. I want to use my hands."

Greta was afraid now. She, whom I'd belonged to ever since I met her that day in Hamburg, met her and gone to pretend illness, to throw up my job, to stay there with her. Yes, I'd belonged to her then, body and soul. I didn't belong to her now. I was myself. I was coming into another kind of kingdom to the one I'd dreamed of.

She was afraid. I loved seeing her afraid and I fastened my hands round her neck. Yes, even now when I am sitting here writing down all about myself (which, mind you, is a very happy thing to do)—to write all about yourself and what you've been through and what you felt and thought and how you deceived everyone—yes, it's wonderful to do. Yes, I was wonderfully happy when I killed Greta. . . .

24

There isn't really very much to say after that. I mean, things came to a climax there. One forgets, I suppose, that there can't be anything better to follow—that you've had it all. I just sat there for a long time. I don't know when they came. I don't know whether they all came at once. . . .

They couldn't have been there all along, because they wouldn't have let me kill Greta. I noticed that God was there first. I don't mean God. I'm confused. I mean Major Phillpot. I'd liked him always; he'd been very nice to me. He was rather like God in some ways, I think—I mean if God had been a human being and not something supernatural—up in the sky somewhere. He was a very fair man—very fair and kind. He looked after things and people. Tried to do his best for people.

I don't know how much he'd known about me. I remember the curious way he looked at me that morning in the sale room when he said that I was "fey." I wonder why he thought I happened to be fey that day?

Then when we were there with that little crumpled heap on the ground that was Ellie in her riding habit. . . . I wonder if he knew then or had some idea that I'd had something to do with it?

After Greta's death, as I say, I just sat there in my chair, staring down at my champagne glass. It was empty. Everything was very empty—very empty indeed. There was just one light that we'd switched on, Greta and I, but it was in the corner. It didn't give much light, and the sun —I think the sun must have set a long time ago. I just say there and wondered what was going to happen next with a sort of dull wonder.

Then, I suppose, the people began coming. Perhaps a lot of people came at once. They came very quietly, if so, or else I wasn't hearing or noticing anybody.

Perhaps if Santonix had been there, he would have told me what to do. Santonix was dead. He'd gone a different way to my way, so he wouldn't be any help. Nobody really would be any help.

After a bit I noticed Dr. Shaw. He was so quiet I hardly knew he was there at first. He was sitting quite near me, just waiting for something. After a while I thought he was waiting for me to speak. I said to him,

"I've come home."

There were one or two other people moving somewhere behind him. They seemed to be waiting—to be waiting for something that he was going to do.

176

"Greta's dead," I said. "I killed her. I expect you'd better take the body away, hadn't you?"

Somebody somewhere let off a flash bulb. It must have been a police photographer photographing the body. Dr. Shaw turned his head and said sharply,

"Not yet."

He turned his head round back to me again. I leaned toward him and said,

"I saw Ellie tonight."

"Did you? Where?"

"Outside standing under a fir tree. It was the place I first saw her, you know." I paused a moment and then said, "She didn't see me. . . . She couldn't see me because I wasn't there." And after a while I said, "That upset me. It upset me very much."

Dr. Shaw said, "It was in the capsule, wasn't it? Cyanide in that capsule? That's what you gave Ellie that morning?"

"It was for her hay fever," I said; "she always took a capsule as a preventive against her allergy when she went riding. Greta and I fixed up one or two of the capsules with wasp stuff from the garden shed and joined them together again. We did it up in the Folly. Smart, wasn't it?" And I laughed. It was an odd sort of laugh. I heard it myself. It was more like a queer little giggle. I said, "You'd examined all the things she took, hadn't you, when you came to see her ankle? Sleeping pills, the allergy capsules, and they were quite all right, weren't they? No harm in any of them."

"No harm," said Dr. Shaw. "They were quite innocent."

"That was rather clever, really, wasn't it?" I said.

"You've been quite clever, yes, but not clever enough."

"All the same, I don't see how you found out."

"We found out when there was a second death—the death you didn't mean to happen."

"Claudia Hardcastle?"

"Yes. She died the same way as Ellie did. She fell from her horse in the hunting field. Claudia was a healthy girl, too, but she just fell from her horse and died. The time wasn't so long there, you see. They picked her up almost at once and there was still the smell of cyanide to go by. If she'd lain in the open air like Ellie for a couple of hours, there'd have been nothing—nothing to smell, nothing to find. I don't see how Claudia got the capsule, though. Unless you'd left one behind in the Folly. Claudia used to go to the Folly sometimes. Her fingerprints were there and she dropped a lighter there."

"We must have been careless. Filling them was rather tricky."

Then I said,

"You suspected I had something to do with Ellie's death, didn't you? All of you?" I looked round at the shadowy figures. "Perhaps all of you."

"Very often one knows. But I wasn't sure whether we'd be able to do anything about it."

"You ought to caution me," I said reprovingly.

"I'm not a police officer," said Dr. Shaw.

"What are you then?"

"I'm a doctor."

"I don't need a doctor," I said.

"That remains to be seen."

I looked at Phillpot then, and I said,

"What are you doing? Come here to judge me, to preside at my trial?"

"I'm only a justice of the peace," he said. "I'm here as a friend."

"A friend of mine?" That startled me.

"A friend of Ellie's," he said.

I didn't understand. None of it made sense to me, but I couldn't help feeling rather important. All of them there! Police and doctors, Shaw and Phillpot, who was a busy man in his way. The whole thing was very complicated. I began to lose count of things. I was very tired, you see. I used to get tired suddenly and go to sleep . . .

And all the coming and going. People came to see me, —all sorts of people. Lawyers, a solicitor, I think, and another kind of lawyer with him and doctors. Several doctors. They bothered me and I didn't want to answer them.

One of them kept asking me if there was anything I

wanted. I said there was. I said there was only one thing I wanted. I said I wanted a ball pen and a lot of paper. I wanted, you see, to write down all about it, how it all came to happen. I wanted to tell them what I'd felt, what I'd thought. The more I thought about myself, the more interesting I thought it would be to everybody. Because I was interesting. I was a really interesting person and I'd done interesting things.

The doctors—one doctor, anyway—seemed to think it was a good idea. I said,

"You always let people make a statement, so why can't I write my statement out? Someday, perhaps, everybody can read it."

They let me do it. I couldn't write very long on end. I used to get tired. Somebody used a phrase like "diminished responsibility," and somebody else disagreed. All sorts of things you hear. Sometimes they don't think you're even listening. Then I had to appear in court and I wanted them to fetch me my best suit because I had to make a good figure there. It seemed they had had detectives watching me for some time. Those new servants. I think they'd been engaged or put on my trail by Lippincott. They found out too many things about me and Greta. Funny, after she was dead, I never thought of Greta much. . . . After I'd killed her, she didn't seem to matter any more.

I tried to bring back the splendid triumphant feeling that I'd had when I strangled her. But even that was gone away. . . .

They brought my mother to see me quite suddenly one day. There she was looking at me from the doorway. She didn't look as anxious as she used to look. I think all she looked now was sad. She hadn't much to say and nor had I. All she said was,

"I tried, Mike. I tried very hard to keep you safe. I failed. I was always afraid that I should fail."

I said, "All right, Mum, it wasn't your fault. I chose to go the way I wanted."

And I thought suddenly, "That's what Santonix said. He was afraid for me, too. He hadn't been able to do any-

179

thing either. Nobody could have done anything—except perhaps I myself. . . . I don't know. I'm not sure. But every now and then I remember—I remember that day when Ellie said to me, "What are you thinking of when you look at me like that?" and I said, "Like what?" She said, "As though you loved me." I suppose in a way I did love her. I could have loved her. She was so sweet, Ellie. Sweet delight . . .

I suppose the trouble with me was that I wanted things too much, always. Wanted them, too, the easy way, the greedy way.

That first time, that first day I came to Gipsy's Acre and met Ellie. As we were going down the road again, we met Esther. It put it into my head that day, the warning she gave Ellie, put it in my head to pay her. I knew she was the kind would do anything for money. I'd pay her. She'd start warning Ellie and frightening her, making her feel that she was in danger. I thought it might make it seem more possible then that Ellie had died from shock. That first day, I know now, I'm sure of it, Esther was really frightened. She was really frightened for Ellie. She warned her, warned her to go away, to have nothing to do with Gipsy's Acre. She was warning her, of course, to have nothing to do with me. I didn't understand that. Ellie didn't understand either.

Was it me Ellie was afraid of? I think it must have been, though she didn't know it herself. She knew there was something threatening her, she knew there was danger. Santonix knew the evil in me, too, just like my mother. Perhaps all three of them knew. Ellie knew but she didn't mind, she never minded. It's odd, very odd. I know now. We were very happy together. Yes, very happy. I wish I'd known then that we were happy. . . . I had my chance. Perhaps everyone has a chance. I—turned my back on it.

It seems odd, doesn't it, that Greta doesn't matter at all?

And even my beautiful house doesn't matter.

Only Ellie . . . And Ellie can never find me again— Endless Night . . . That's the end of my story.

In my end is my beginning—that's what people are always saying.

But what does it mean?

And just where does my story begin? I must try and think. . . .